THE
*U*NWELCOME *A*NGEL

An emotionally gripping wartime novella

CHRISSIE BRADSHAW

VALLUM PUBLISHING

Published by Vallum Publishing

All enquiries to vallumpublishing@gmail.com

Cover design by: JD Smith

Dedication

To all NHS workers past and present who have done so much for so many.

PROLOGUE

Linwood Colliery, Northumberland 1944

Linwood nestles in a dale surrounded by farmland that stretches all the way to the sandy beaches of Northumberland and, on the horizon, you can see the North Sea blend into wide skies. A patchwork carpet of allotments sits behind the five rows of colliery houses that lead up to the pit head.

Rolling fells rise behind the pit wheel giving it a backdrop of dark green. The railway line that transports the coal is flanked on either side by hedges that flower throughout summer and give up a harvest of blackberries, sloe berries and rosehips in autumn.

The tiny hive of industry that is Linwood Colliery has been carved from a once tranquil beauty spot because, hidden far below the fields and fells lie great riches. Seam after seam of black gold runs under land and sea waiting to be mined.

In every Linwood household there is at least one miner who is vital to the country's fight for freedom. Every day, he mines coal to keep the factories running, to keep the forces in action and to keep the home fires burning for when the troops come back from war. At the heart of every Linwood home there is another fighter who must feed a working man and a family on wartime rations, keep them clothed and fight against pit dust and disease.

1

Ginnie Kelly sat down at the kitchen table of number one First Row with her cup of strong black tea and a pen and paper. The three bairns were playing down the row just outside the Simpsons' house. It was a cold Saturday morning but being outdoors would do them good. Her daughter, Rose and the twins were wrapped up in scarves and gloves although Stanley was a little imp and never kept his on for long. With John, her husband, working at his allotment for the morning, this was the ideal time to sit and work out what to do with the pile of coupons and jar of coins they had set aside for Christmas.

Mary-from-next-door, her elderly friend, was fond of saying that you couldn't make a silk purse out of a sow's ear but Ginnie Kelly was stubborn enough to try. She would make 1944 a silk purse of a Christmas they'd all remember. The war with its rationing and shortages and eking out a pitman's wages didn't make preparing for Christmas easy but Ginnie knew plenty of families in Linwood Colliery rows who were far worse off. Not all of her neighbours had a good man like hers who willingly tipped up his pay. John Kelly was happy to leave their housekeeping to Ginnie's thrifty management and she wouldn't let him down.

Top of her list of expenses was the home-reared chicken that she'd already ordered from Mr Dodd in Fifth Row. He always fattened a few up on his allotment for Christmas. All the veg would come from John's efforts. He went to the allotment to sketch and paint when he got the chance so his shed held more canvases and paint than gardening tools but he grew enough to keep them going with potatoes, carrots and greens.

Rose had already given her a list of books she would like to read and asked if she would pick one out. Ginnie knew she couldn't go wrong with the new Enid Blyton that headed the list; some mystery about a disappearing cat. Ginnie had a mind to buy a hank of new cream wool to mix in with the spare blue she already had. She'd knit her daughter a new cardigan on the quiet after Rose went to bed. Rose loved a surprise.

Just this week, the twins had discussed what they were going to ask for in their letter to Father Christmas and, after deciding that even old 'ho ho' wouldn't be able to get two bikes during the war, they'd settled on soldier figures and a *Beano* annual. Ginnie counted out what was in the jar and was happy to discover that she might manage those too. That left sock wool for John. That man of hers quickly went through his thick pit socks until they were more darns than sole. Would her coupons cover that much wool?

The back door burst open startling her as she counted out coupons. 'What's the matter lassie? You've nearly taken the door off its hinges!'

Rose stood in the doorway, rosy-cheeked and wide-eyed. 'Lottie's mam, she's sent us all away from her back yard. She said to us, "All of you get back to your own rows and you'd better not call around until I tell your mams we're clear." The twins have come back to this end of the row, too. They're playing outside Mary-from-next-door's house.'

'Have Edna Simpson's lads got nits again? They keep playing with those Irwins and their heads are always lifting.' Ginnie got up to get her nit comb from the drawer. 'I'd better give you a comb through, pet.'

'No Mam, it's not nits. She told me, "Rose, you go home now and tell your mam our Sid is proper poorly and going to the isolation hospital." Why is Sid going there? What's wrong with him, Mam?'

An icy feeling clenched at the pit of Ginnie's stomach. She shivered and pulled her cardigan around her. The children's isolation hospital? It had to be the strangling angel. There had been a case or two in Burnside, the neighbouring village, and it was Sid's grandma who had raised the alarm along these rows just last week.

One of Granny Simpson's lodgers had brought it into Burnside and he'd been taken to hospital a week ago. That poor bairn had been at his granny's at the time. Ginnie went to the back door and called, 'David, Stanley... in now!'

Like well-trained whippets, the two came scooting through the gate into the yard, Stanley without his gloves and David with a bloody knee. *Who would have boys?* Ginnie thought as she grabbed one by the collar to face the gate and pushed the other towards the scullery door. 'Stanley, back down the row and find your gloves or there's no dinner for you. David get to the sink so I can clean up that knee, look at the state of the pair of you.'

Ginnie heated water on the range in preparation for an early bath time then bundled all of their outdoor clothes into the outbuilding that stood in the yard. Their outhouse had two doors side by side and a window. Behind one door was the coal shed and the other opened onto a washhouse-come-netty. Housed at one end was the netty, a modern one that flushed, and at the other was a bench with a deep sink, a copper boiler for heating water, a poss tub and a mangle.

Only the end houses of each row had outhouses of this size in their yard and Ginnie was proud of it. She kept it tidy, kept the net curtain at the window white and whitewashed the walls every spring. She placed the bundle on the bench thinking she'd scrub the life out of those clothes with carbolic soap then put them in the poss tub with a good handful of Oxydol to get rid of any germs on Monday, washing day.

Their tin bath was hung on a nail in the wall, beside the bench. She took it down, carried it into the kitchen and set it down by the fire. She arranged the three sided wooden clothes horse, used for drying clothes on wet wash days, around the bath and put towels over it to give Rose, who was ten, a bit of privacy from the twins. Rose would get the clean water and the twins, wrestling around the floor in just their underpants, would jump in after her.

Once they were clean, they'd stay in their siren suits, the warm all-in-ones she had made out of old blankets for them to pop on to go to the Anderson shelter when the siren wailed in the middle of the night. Their Sunday clothes were hanging ready for tomorrow.

Yes, on Monday, she'd put that bundle in as hot a wash as she could get away with without shrinking the jumpers. The strangling angel was highly infectious and Ginnie had an uncommon fear of doctors and hospitals so her head chattered with 'what ifs?'. What if her twins were next? They played with Sid every day. How long would that little bairn be away from his mother? What if he took a turn for the worse?

Ginnie calmed herself by staying busy and making two corned beef and potato pies. One for themselves and one for the Simpsons. Edna Simpson still had a few mouths to feed and a pie wouldn't go amiss. John could take it along and leave it with their good wishes when he got home from the allotment.

Later that afternoon while they tucked into their warm pie served with a good dollop of mushy peas, David piped up, 'Sid kept sneezing all week but his mam made him go to school with Lottie and Alfie. He was all hot on Friday after school and he hadn't even been running about. He tried to play Tommies and Jerries with us but he had no breath and went inside before he was called. Will he be away long, Mam?'

Ginnie wished she'd known all this before she'd let the boys go out to play with him yesterday just for an hour before their tea. The Simpsons went to the catholic school in the next village so her lads had only been with him that one hour after school then with his brother, Alfie, this morning. 'He'll be away as long as it takes to get better. Eat your pie crust, David.'

'I wish I was off school for a bit. Maybe we'll catch it, David,' Stanley pinched David's crust off his plate and ate it for him. She couldn't fill Stanley but David was a picky eater.

Ginnie didn't want to scare the boys but wanted to put them straight. 'It's not a bit of fun and a way to stay off school, our Stanley. This is all we need in the rows. If it's not one thing, it's another.'

John put his knife and fork down. 'Sit down and drink your tea and try a bit of this pie lass. Fretting never changed a thing.' She could read John's look; he didn't want her worrying the bairns, so she sat at the table.

Ginnie sipped her tea but she knew the tight knot in her chest wouldn't make way for a bit of pie.

'What is it exactly, this thing he's got then, Mam?' Rose asked.

'We've called it the strangling angel since I was a lass. Its rightful name is diphtheria and it comes and goes. There's a vaccination programme going on because it's on the rise again but, you might guess, there's been no sight or smell of the vaccine around here.'

'I thought he just had a cold. I haven't heard of any of the folks in the rows going down with the strangling angel but it sounds scary.' Rose looked from her mam's worried face to her dad.

'It's no laughing matter but don't worry, lass.' John Kelly tried to calm Rose. 'Isolation means Sid is being taken away to stop it spreading. Until we're sure it's contained, you mustn't go near their house or see Lottie. That'll keep us all safe.'

'I hope so John.' Ginnie cleared the plates and prayed her husband was right.

2

Edna Simpson sat in front of the range knitting pit socks on four needles. It was second nature to her so she didn't need to look at what she was doing but the clicking sound and finding something to keep her hands busy comforted her. Her mind was racing. What was happening to her bairn now? Were they keeping him comfortable? Was he crying for her?

She blamed herself. She should have kept Sid off school at his first sneeze. It was November though and they'd all had coughs and sneezes of some sort that month. How was she to know the angel would sneak in through his granny's back door?

She blamed her mother-in-law. Why had Granny Simpson decided to take on a couple of Bevin boys as lodgers? One lad had brought another unwelcome lodger with him after a trip home for a wedding. He'd come back with a sore throat and a fever and brought the strangling bleeding angel into their midst.

The doctor knew what he had straight away because the illness brings a sweet, sickly scent to the breath. He was taken to hospital but by then he'd spread his germs, hadn't he? He'd given them to her boy.

She blamed Sid. Hadn't he yammered on and on to stay at Granny Simpson's last weekend? He'd been eager to hear tales from the Bevin boy when he got back from the East End of London.

She blamed the Bevin boy. That was the start of it. He had been best man for his soldier brother and Sid wanted to hear about London and the soldiers. Edna put her knitting aside and rolled her shoulders. She had to stop this, it was nobody's fault. It was just another enemy to land on their doorstep.

Her Bert had gone out an hour ago to drown his sorrows at the 'tute. The working men's institute was his escape and she didn't begrudge him that time to himself. In the peace and quiet of her kitchen, she let the tears flow and felt sorry for every clout around the ear she had given that lad of hers. He was a handful but he was her handful and, at six years old, he was fighting against the strangling angel all by himself and miles away. She loved every hair of his head, even when he came home nit-riddled from playing with the Irwins. She ached to hold him, to scold him and to have him home.

Edna took herself off to bed before Bert came home even though she'd never sleep. The drink would have made Bert maudlin and she had enough on her own mind to cope with. She'd say her rosary and pray for Sid and the Bevin boy, he was only nineteen after all, to be spared from the strangling angel.

On Monday, Granny Simpson arrived with cleaning cloths and her scrubbing bush and Edna felt her ears turn red as she thought about the blame she'd placed upon her mother-in-law. Granny brought news that Ron, the Bevin boy had a name, was recovering but would be convalescing back in London when he left the hospital.

'It'll be best if he starts at another colliery when he is fit enough to work. Folk in Burnside have long memories,' she said giving Edna a long look. 'The lad wasn't happy to move north to mine coal instead of joining his brothers in the army. Luck of the draw, though.'

'I hope his family don't go thinking that he got the diphtheria from us. It was travelling to that wedding I'm sure,' Edna sniffed.

Granny Simpson cleaned the house and watched the two lads while Edna tackled the week's washing with Lottie and Eileen. All of the Simpsons had to stay off school for a few days in case they'd been kissed by the strangling angel too, so she was putting the girls to work.

They got the week's wash out on the lines that zig-zagged the yard by early afternoon, but Granny Simpson stayed to see her son, who was upstairs sleeping after a night shift, and help make their dinner. They all loved her dumplings and gravy and it gave Edna time to make a start on the ironing. She had three irons on the go, two warming on the range and one in her hand, so the small kitchen was like a furnace.

As she tackled Bert's shirts, Edna couldn't help saying, 'Well Mam, maybe you'll think twice about opening your doors to folk who aren't family.'

Granny Simpson was having none of that. 'I'm doing my bit for the war. We're short of miners because our lads are join-ing the forces and the government have solved the shortage by bringing in Bevin boys but they still need somewhere to live. We don't have enough in the area to build a barracks for them.'

'Ron didn't want to be a Bevin boy so why was he here?' Alfie Simpson asked.

Granny Simpson looked towards Bert, who had got up because of the noise the household was making and had grumpily settled at the table with the paper. 'Bert, you explain to the lad instead of burying your nose in that paper. Reading about the ins and outs of the war can wait.'

Bert sighed but closed the paper and Edna smiled to her-self. That was him told.

'It's like this, son. At the end of last year it started, ten percent of all males, that's one out of ten, were consigned to the mines instead of the forces.'

'Why's that, Dad?' Alfie frowned.

'Too many of our own young lads wanted to join up and fight the war so we hadn't enough miners left.'

'We need them here,' Alfie said. 'So why are the miners always grumbling about them?'

'Wait a minute, I'll come to that. As I was saying, ten percent have become miners, Bevin boys we call them, due to Ernest Bevin, he's our minister for labour and national service. Not many of the ten percent are happy about it. For a start, it's dirty and dangerous work, there's no uniform or medals for a miner and young lads want to fight for their country. What's worse, because conscientious objectors, I've told you before about the Connies, have previously been consigned to the pits, some of Bevin's boys feel they're all looked on with suspicion for trying to avoid the war.'

'You can't blame them for feeling unwanted, Dad. You lot are always slagging off the Bevin boys.' Lottie joined in.

'You're right and you're wrong Lottie lass. The miners aren't keen on working with Bevin boys but it's nothing to do with thinking they're all Connies. The truth is we don't think they are trained enough to work with us. Four weeks of training is a farce. They're okay up top I suppose, but down below? That's where your marras hold your life in their hands. Trust takes years of families working together, handpicking our deputies and shotfirers and getting to know the smells and sounds that warn you of danger. Unwilling conscripts don't make great workmates.'

'We need the coal brought up so you have to give them a chance.' Granny Simpson sniffed as she put on her coat. 'That Bevin boy, Ron, he'd do any job for me and willingly. My other Bevin chap, Matt, he's as strong as an ox; farming stock. He fills the coal scuttle and tips up his board without me asking. That's more than can be said of my sons when they were home. Our Sid likes the lads because they listen to him and give him some attention.' Edna widened her eyes and caught Lottie's stifled grin. Granny Simpson was the only one who could get away with scolding Bert.

As she reached the door, Granny added, 'I'm off to see

Matt, the one I've got left, and a nicer young man you couldn't find. He shared a room with Ron so I hope he's not smitten. Enjoy those dumplings.'

Edna made Bert a cup of tea before he went to his shift. He'd sat quietly with the paper in his hands all night. 'I've made us a brew before you set off. You're very quiet Bert?' She placed the tea by his side.

'Maybe she was right, my mother. I haven't given the lad enough attention. The times he's asked me to play football in the street or to take him fishing, and the times I've said no.' Bert put his head in his hands.

What could she say? It was true but Edna felt a pang of sympathy for Bert. He worked hard so an afternoon's fishing and the 'tute were his reward for a gruelling week. 'Remember that when he's better, Bert. Maybe you could fix your old rod for him and let him try?'

3

The angel stretched its wings to swoop through Sid's catholic school in the next village as Ginnie waited for it to claim its next victim in Linwood Colliery rows. Would it pay a visit to their little elementary school? Ginnie's insides churned as she prayed for this to pass and watched the twins for any sign of fever.

One of Sid's pals from Third Row was next and there was talk about the vaccine coming around to them all soon. Their area was like the cow's tail, it always came last.

School ran as usual but the teachers kept the windows open and had the children out in the fresh air at playtime. The classes were much smaller because, if anyone had a sore throat or cough, they had to call the doctor out straight away and all the children in the family had to stay off school.

A few lads and lasses had the doctor to them but it turned out they were 'putting it on' and got into trouble because a doctor's visit cost money whether you were ill or not.

Ginnie had been so pre-occupied with dark thoughts about needing to call the doctor that the week of Rose's trial exam came as a surprise to her. Already? How would she do?

Their Rose was clever, one of the brightest ten-year-olds Miss Wakenshaw had ever taught, so she said. The school wanted her to enter the entrance exam for a scholarship place at the girls' high school in the market town of Morpeth. This was unheard of in the rows but when Miss Wakenshaw had explained that, after the war, the new education act would make further schooling an option for everyone, John thought it seemed sensible to let Rose give the entrance exam a try.

Ginnie wasn't so sure herself and she'd said so to the teacher and to John. She felt more reserved about it because, even with a scholarship, they'd have to provide uniform and bus fare. What an expense that would be. Her other worry was, what if she got above herself and it spoilt the lovely lassie she was?

Miss Wakenshaw and the headmaster thought two pupils in the class stood a chance of going on to high school; Rose and Douglas Fletcher, the under-manager's son. They were going to do practice papers in the headmaster's room to see if they should take the proper exam for a scholarship next term. Mr Brown, the headmaster, wanted to make sure that anyone he entered for the exam would do his school proud.

Douglas would go to King Edward's at whatever level he passed because his parents were willing to pay fees for their only son. Ginnie had the feeling that Mrs Fletcher came from monied folk and an under-manager took home a good wage. Their Rose's only chance of getting into the girls' school was to get a really high grade and win a scholarship place, and they were as rare as Ginnie finding a banana for sale in the greengrocer's shop.

Ginnie could see that Rose was excited when the day of the practice test came. 'Just do your best, pet and, if you don't do well there is no shame in it because you'll have tried.'

'I think I will do well, Mam. It's reading, writing and arithmetic and I'm top at all of them.'

Ginnie smiled as Rose set off full of self-confidence. Where did she get it from?

There were two papers. One before lunch and one after. Ginnie had Rose's lunchtime sandwich ready for her and Mary-from-next-door popped in to hear how the morning had gone.

'What a morning!' Rose said as she sat to eat her lunch, and Ginnie searched her face for signs that it had gone well.

'How did it go then? We're on tenterhooks.' Mary asked.

'The test was fine but we had such a palaver! Sit down Mam and pour the tea and I'll tell you.'

Ginnie poured herself a strong black cup and added a dash of milk into Rose's. 'I'm all ears.'

'We had to go to the sir's office, me and Douglas, and Douglas looked like a ghost. "Are you worried about this?" I asked him.

'"I'm not worried about the test, it's just a practice, but I don't feel well," he told me. "Mam didn't believe me. She said it was just nerves and it was too important to miss so I had to come."

'We started the paper and it had lots of straightforward arithmetic and then lots of mathematical problems about men digging holes and the time it took to travel from one place to another. I got right to the end before I glanced across at Douglas who had his head on his desk. He seemed to be asleep. I shouted, 'Sir!' and Mr Brown glared at me over his glasses.

'"No talking until the test is over, Rose."

'"I've finished, sir, but look at Douglas. He said he didn't feel well."

'Mr Brown walked over to Douglas and shook him by the elbow.

'"Douglas, lad what's wrong?"

'Douglas wasn't right, he let out a groan and sir said, "Rose. Go quickly to Miss Wakenshaw and send her to me. You stay and watch her class of infants. You're a sensible girl so read them a story until you hear the lunchtime bell and then send them out."

'So that's what I did.' She gulped at her tea. 'Now I have to go back and do the second part.'

'I hope it's not the strangling angel and you've been sitting with him all morning,' Mary held her apron to her mouth in horror.

'Calm down, Mary. Rose has another test this afternoon and the lad might just have exam fright. Mrs Fletcher would know if the lad was sickening for anything like that.' Ginnie's chest tightened and she struggled to breathe without gasping, she'd had the same thought as Mary but she didn't want to frighten Rose.

Rose happily returned to school to answer a paper of comprehension questions, correcting spellings and putting some punctuation right. Ginnie tried to keep busy and cleaned out the dresser to occupy herself but it didn't stop her imagining the worst.

The news spread like nits at a party. Douglas Fletcher had been whisked off to the isolation hospital. Ginnie got the boiler going in the outhouse and used the poss tub even though it wasn't wash day. A thorough hot wash for everything Rose had worn on the day of the test. Panic invaded every bit of her body, she felt hot then cold and she felt shaky, but she stayed outwardly calm. She squeezed Rose's clothes through the mangle and hung them out to dry determined to keep the strangling angel at bay. It wasn't getting its toe over the threshold of number one First Row.

4

Working in the children's isolation hospital was hard work but Helen Tweedie loved it. She had always wanted to be a nurse and she knew she was good at it. Working with sick children and seeing them get well was the best job in the world, except for when… she quickly dismissed the dark side of doing her job.

Her duties were on the boys' diphtheria ward and, this month, it seemed like she had half the boys in Burnside and its neighbouring village of Linwood in her care. One or two were really critical and in side rooms with a nurse to themselves but most of them were doing well. With luck, a handful would be home for Christmas.

Diphtheria struck the young more than adults and there was no telling whether it would take a hold or release its strangling grasp on the youngsters in her care. There was no getting away from it, diphtheria was a killer. There was a vaccine now and she had had it so that she could work in the hospital. It was being rolled out to all the nation's children. They had made a start in the larger cities but it hadn't reached half the children in the country so they had a long way to go before it was eradicated.

The disease was highly infectious, spread by coughs and sneezes, so the patients had to be isolated from their family until all evidence of it was gone. Parents could visit and look through the large window into the ward from the corridor on a Saturday but, other than that, they had no news of their children. Helen thought it must be a terrible time for them. Parents seldom had phones and, even if they did, calls were limited to emergencies so the only clue they had was reading the hospital news in the evening paper.

November 16th 1944

Children's isolation
hospital diphtheria wards

Boys 4 recovering 14 stable
4 critical 0 deaths

Girls 6 recovering 11 stable
2 critical 1 death

Imagine reading that? The relief if you had a son and the terror if you had a daughter. Waiting for a telegram. Waiting and dreading that knock on the door. Counting the hours until Saturday visiting and wondering whether your child was one of the critical ones.

Helen took over her duties from the night shift and read the updated notes on Sidney Simpson. He'd been moved to a side ward and was finding it hard to breathe. His throat had swollen to give him the bull neck of a patient who was really poorly and his notes showed that his temperature was dangerously high. Yes, Sidney was critical.

She brushed back the mop of blonde hair plastered to his brow and decided on a sponge down to cool him off. As she headed for the door to collect a bowl of water, she spotted a figure looking through the window. It wasn't Saturday but relatives sometimes tried to sneak a peek of their loved ones through the week, and who could blame them.

Approaching the window, she half expected the figure to scarper as many did, in case they got into trouble, but this man stayed and rewarded her with a smile.

'I'm looking for Sid Simpson. I've peered through every window and couldn't find him,' he mouthed through the glass.

Helen wasn't sure whether to reveal that the lad in the bed was Sid or not. His parents didn't know he was critical yet because, when she'd met them last Saturday, he was poorly but he wasn't swollen like this. This tall dark-haired chap wasn't the father. 'Who are you?' she enquired.

The man drew up closer to the window 'I'm Matt, Matt Wilson. I lodge with Sid Simpson's grandmother in Burnside.'

A lodger; that explained his different accent. Helen knew she couldn't give information to anyone other than the parents but this man had obviously travelled far and infiltrated the hospital grounds to take news to Sid's granny. It wouldn't be good news and she couldn't let his parents know like this. 'I'm sorry we can't divulge patient information and this is a side ward for a poorly young lad so you'll have to leave.'

'Sorry. I'll move away.' The man disappeared and Helen breathed a sigh of relief. It would be four more days before Mr and Mrs Simpson discovered that Sidney was one of the critically ill.

She was filling a bowl at the sluice station when there was a knock at the window above the sink and the face appeared again. 'Sorry to bother you but can I tell Granny Simpson her grandson is doing okay? She's blaming herself and not sleeping.'

Helen admired his determination but what could she say? No, he's not doing okay? That wouldn't help anybody but she couldn't send false hope either. 'Look Matt, you can tell his grandmother that you couldn't find him and all the boys are asleep for the night.'

'That's the best you can do?'

'It is.'

'Thank you, nurse.' He smiled and was gone.

He was handsome and looked to be in his twenties. Why wasn't Granny Simpson's lodger in the forces? Helen's attention was soon taken by the ward sister calling, 'Nurse Tweedie, we need your help on the main ward.'

It was going to be a busy shift.

Helen didn't notice darkness falling until it was time to draw the blackout curtains. Her aching feet and rumbling stomach informed her that her shift was almost over. There was just time for one last call in to Sid to check his temperature. He looked no better but his temperature hadn't risen any higher. 'Hang on in there, Sid. I'll see you tomorrow.' Poor little lad. She braced herself to call in on two more of her patients who were just as ill so she could update their reports for the day staff.

5

Mid-week and the house was quiet except for the ticking of the kitchen clock. Dorothy Fletcher watched the clock as she stirred the soup that was simmering on the range. The clock's hands moved so slowly. Since Douglas was rushed to hospital, she had seen him only once through a window looking into his ward for a minute or two on Saturday. There was another four hours before she could see her boy. How would she fill in the minutes?

She lifted the soup to one side to stay warm for when Neville came home and wiped a tear from her eye. She couldn't give in to another bout of crying and go to the hospital red-eyed. She must keep busy.

Taking a duster and polish from the kitchen, she headed upstairs to polish her already dustless bedroom. She paused at Douglas's bedroom door. It was ajar as it always was and she'd give anything to pop her head around and ask him what he was making.

She walked through the doorway and sat on his bed. His Meccano kit was on the desk, with something half-made and abandoned. She picked up a long metal rod and squeezed it tightly to stop the tears. He was always constructing something was Douglas. Neville wanted him to be an engineer.

On the bookcase there were books about building, about science, about animals. Didn't he love finding out about things?

A few comics sat on top of an exercise book. She picked up the book and flicked through the pages of arithmetic and spellings that Neville had set for Douglas, extra work so that he had a good chance of passing that entrance exam. Why oh why hadn't she listened to him that day when he had told her he was ill? She had sent him off just to sit a silly practice test.

The tears flooded down her cheeks, she could hold them back no longer. They didn't even help. They weren't healing tears, just scalding tears of blame and regret. She covered her face with her hands, why had she sent Douglas into school thinking he had exam nerves? She hadn't listened to her boy. She hadn't dreamed he had been anywhere near the Irwins and caught diphtheria. She was his mother. How couldn't she know?

It was Mrs Irwin who told her that he'd met her boys and gone fishing down by the burn a few days before Tommy Irwin came down with diphtheria. The burn was swollen with the rain and fast-flowing, and he'd been warned not to go there.

Douglas knew for days that two of the Irwin boys were in the isolation hospital but he hadn't told her about playing with them by the burn. Was he frightened he'd get into trouble for being there, for being around them or was he trying to save her from worry? She couldn't ask him because he was so poorly and they could only see him through the window of his ward.

This wouldn't do. Dorothy went into her bedroom and dabbed at her eyes. She would put on fresh powder and lipstick and get changed into the suit that was Douglas's favourite. He loved green. He was such a lovely lad and she was blessed having him.

Dorothy didn't like to think of the disappointments and 'misses' she'd had to endure before she eventually gave birth to Douglas. They had been married five years before he arrived and there had been two misses afterwards too. She was almost forty so it seemed like he'd be their only child. He was enough. He was everything to them and she just prayed he'd pull through this.

Neville was under-manager at Linwood colliery and they were lucky to have a car so, when he got home, they'd travel into the countryside to look through the outside window into Douglas's ward before darkness fell. He was unwell and wouldn't know they were there but she really needed this extra visit as well as the official one that they were allowed on Saturday. She just had to see her boy.

Her head was running a constant prayer, 'Please Lord, save my boy. Please Lord, let me hold him again soon.'

Neville hadn't been keen on flouting the rules but he'd given in to her. It was Bert Simpson, his son Sid was at the hospital, who'd told Neville about the gap in the fencing and he'd mentioned that a few parents made the odd trip just to set their minds at rest. Once Dorothy knew, she wanted to pay an extra visit straight away.

'I'm not going to make a habit of this, Dorothy. Just this once,' he said as he parked the car by the locked hospital gates. As they left the country lane to find the gap, the light was fading. They'd have to be quick or the blackout curtains would be drawn and they'd miss catching sight of Douglas.

They crossed the lawn and found the outside windows of Douglas's ward. Dorothy's heart thudded as she stood on tiptoe to peek through into the ward. Douglas's bed was empty. She counted four down again to make sure. She scanned every other bed to see his familiar mop of red hair, but no.

'Neville, I can't find him,' she whispered and stood aside to let Neville check. 'Can you see him, Neville?' Her teeth chattered. Was it the cold or fear?

Neville moved from the window and took her in his arms. 'You're shivering, darling. Maybe they've changed wards. He definitely isn't here.'

'We have to knock on the door. We have to find out. His bed is empty. What if?' She gasped for breath. 'Oh Neville, why isn't he there?'

Neville led her away from the window, dusk would soon change to pitch darkness and he was leading her back to the car. She pulled away. 'Neville we must go to the main entrance and ask what's going on.'

Neville gripped both shoulders. 'Dorothy I should never have brought you. Now you'll worry more than ever until Saturday. We arc trespassing and we shouldn't be here so let's go home and wait for news.'

Dorothy turned towards the hospital. The blackout curtains were being pulled and the place was disappearing before her eyes. It melted into the darkness and she stumbled as she walked over toward the entrance. Neville took her hand. 'It's dark darling. The staff are busy and nobody will thank you for arriving uninvited. Rules are rules. They have them to stop this sort of panic. Let's go home.'

What if the matron had been trying to phone and they weren't home? The hospital knew they had a telephone and had taken their number. The evening paper would be sitting on the mat and it would have the latest figures from the hospital. She couldn't wait to get home yet she dreaded it. What if the paper recorded a death? What if they'd missed a call? What if a telegram was waiting?

6

Every morning before school, Ginnie gave Rose a dose of special tonic that cost a shilling from the chemist but, a few days later, she was woken in the night.

She felt a tapping on her shoulder then, 'Mam, wake up!'

Ginnie sat up in the darkness. 'What is it, pet? There's no siren tonight.'

'You'll have to send for the doctor, Mam. I've got the diphtheria.'

Ginnie heard the croak in her daughter's voice and put the back of her hand on Rose's fevered brow. It wasn't a nightmare, it was real. She couldn't let it happen. She couldn't lose her lassie, couldn't leave her in the hands of strangers in a hospital.

Ginnie cradled Rose, lanky as she was, in her lap. The doctor confirmed the obvious, Rose had diphtheria. He went off to summon the ambulance and Ginnie resigned herself to the inevitable horror; Rose would be sent to the isolation hospital for several weeks. Several weeks without her firstborn, weeks where her life might hang in the balance. Ginnie stroked Rose's damp brow and tried to pour all of her love and strength into her. 'I'll pray that you'll be looked after my love and you'll come home,' she whispered.

'Sing a hymn, Mam,' Rose croaked and Ginnie was crooning, 'How Great Thou Art' into Rose's ear as she heard the ambulance pull up. She clutched her daughter tightly and closed her eyes and kept on singing as the chill November wind rushed in through the open door. Rose stirred and murmured and she hushed her, 'Shush shush my pet lamb, you just rest.'

John's arms lifted Rose firmly out of hers. Ginnie wanted to clutch her back but she knew she had no choice but to let him carry her to the waiting vehicle. 'I'm going with her. She won't go there alone. I'll see her into the place then I'll walk back,' he said.

Ginnie stared into the dying embers of the fire. They were miles from the hospital and her man had a shift in the morning. She turned and took his face in her hands. 'Thanks John. Stay with her for as long as you can.'

The door closed but November left its chill in the room. Ginnie took a thick cardigan, the one she wore when they needed to use the Anderson shelter, from a peg on the back of the door. She picked up the coal scuttle and revived the fire. She couldn't go to bed, it would be a long night and she would make sure John had a hot breakfast and a cup of tea waiting for him before going down the pit.

After putting the kettle on the hob to boil, she sat back in the chair and listened to the silence. The fire crackling, the clock ticking but there was stillness in her head. It had stopped its incessant yammering at last. It had nothing to yammer to her about because it had happened, her worst fear since the angel came to Linwood colliery. It was trying to steal one of her bairns from her. This nothing, this numbness, she hoped it would last a while because she knew only too well what the pain would be like when it wore off.

John knew a bit about Ginnie's fears. Of course he did because he was her husband. A phobia, he called it because he read a lot and liked to use the right word for everything. She didn't know if this feeling was a phobia but the depth of it and the panic it caused inside her was nobody's pain but her own.

Such fear and panic of doctors, hospitals and the like, it was to do with her family and she couldn't shake it off. *God knows I've tried*, she thought as she took the kettle from the range to add hot water to the teapot.

She'd used Mary-from-next-door and a midwife for the babies but, other than that, she had avoided having anything to do with doctors, nurses and hospitals, the people who had taken her mother and her sister from her. She had kept her family healthy and hadn't let anyone get their hands on any of them, until now.

Ginnie took a photo album from the dresser cupboard and sat at the table with it. The first photograph was brown and faded but it showed her grandmother with two little girls, her mother and aunt. This grandmother had died young of 'women's troubles' so she'd heard.

Her own mother became ill when Ginnie was eight. When Ginnie was older she found out that her mother had been diagnosed with cancer in her breast and was determined to bring up Ginnie and her brothers and sisters, so she had undergone a radical treatment. Ginnie could remember Mam coming home after the removal of her breast and chest muscles and being unable to use her right arm.

Mam had explained that she didn't mind the pain, or the loss of the use of her arm, because her operation meant she'd be able to see them all grow up and marry. She didn't though, her mother went through all of that suffering and died just before Ginnie was ten.

Dad was angry. He was sure that cancers grew once the air got to them and swore that his wife should never have been cut open. He believed it shortened her life when she thought it would save her. Ginnie's fear of doctors and dentists interfering with her started then. She could never have an operation.

She had very few pictures of her mother but she looked like her. Would she carry the family disease? Her sister had.

She came to a photo of herself with Elsie. A few years

older, Elsie had been a second mother to her and her brothers. She'd lost Elsie to cancer of the breast when Rose was just a little'un and she was expecting the twins. There was no way that Ginnie could go to the hospital to visit her but she came home and they had shared many hours together before the end.

Ginnie was certain she had every chance of ending up the same way as the other women in her family so that decided her. She would finish adding to her family because she didn't want to leave more young ones and land Rose with the job of raising lots of children and staying at home. Elsie, who raised her and all of her brothers, had had no life of her own.

Thankfully John had agreed to this. 'You're going nowhere bonny lass but the bairns we have are enough for me. I'll make sure you don't fall again.'

All this worry about the curse on the women in the family, all this worry of leaving Rose with the twins and her father to look after, all this worry about passing the curse on to Rose, and look at what had happened. That bleeding strangling angel had slipped in and snatched her daughter right from under her nose. First the war and now diphtheria, if it wasn't one thing, it was another.

Ginnie came to the photos of her wedding day and her bairns as babies. She closed the album before salt tears could ruin the pages. The yammering was starting again, her head was whirring with 'what ifs'. What if her daughter didn't come home? What if the twins came down next? It didn't bear thinking about.

She examined her breasts for lumps regularly and, so far, nothing. Thank the lord she was clear of that curse for now but she'd gladly swap if it would bring her daughter home. Are you listening God? Spare my daughter.

7

The Simpson household was always a noisy busy one in the mornings and this Saturday was no exception. Edna was finishing off a pie to leave for the bairns while she went to the hospital, boiling a ham and making pease pudding for their meal tonight and trying to sort out what Eileen, Lottie and Alfie would do for the afternoon while she was out.

'Alfie, you can play in the back yard. Back yard only, no mixing, I don't want any more diphtheria entering this house. Do you hear me?'

'Mam! That's not fair. It's Saturday. We're all clear, you said so. Can I go to play with David and Stanley along the row? Pleeease.' Alfie, just seven, tugged at her apron and gave her his winning toothy grin.

'No. Their mam won't want you there and neither do I. It's the yard or nothing.'

'Stop yammering or I'll scalp you.' Bert Simpson came downstairs dressed in his Sunday best even though it was a Saturday.

'Let's come with you, then,' Alfie asked.

'Children aren't allowed, pet,' Edna explained as she put the pie into the oven and checked that the ham that was simmering in a pot over the fire hadn't gone dry.

Lottie was washing the breakfast dishes and Eileen was drying. 'Can we take Alfie for a walk down by the burn this afternoon, Mam?' Eileen asked.

Edna frowned. They'd be planning to meet their friends accidently on purpose. 'As long as you go over the fields, wear your wellies, stick to your three selves and go near nobody else.'

'We mix all day at school, Mam. What's different about Saturdays?' Lottie dried her hands and started putting dishes on the scullery shelf.

Edna was thinking they had a point seeing as the school was staying open and they had to go there. Was she being fair asking them not to see their friends? Bert saved her from answering. Discussions weren't his strong point but thinking up punishments that the kids knew he would never carry out were.

'Do as your mother says or I swear that three heads will roll by the end of the day.' Bert puffed on his pipe and glanced at his pocket watch. 'Edna we have fifteen minutes before leaving for the bus. Will you be ready, hinny?'

Edna drew a deep breath, 'Just. If you girls keep an eye on the oven and the hob and keep Alfie occupied, we'll use some coupons to get you a quarter of sweets from Norris's shop on the way home.'

'Each?' asked Lottie.

Edna tutted, 'No, to share,' as she rushed upstairs to smarten herself up. She'd brush her hair, put on some lipstick and powder and wear her best tweed coat.

They got off the bus near the hospital with Granny Simpson, who'd boarded at Burnside. Her mother-in-law had an orange and a comic for Sid but Edna wasn't sure when he'd be well enough to enjoy those. She hadn't brought a thing. She wanted to see him sitting up and well before she tempted fate and brought him a gift. She did have a card drawn by Alfie and signed by them all though.

'Eeh, it's a long walk up this drive,' panted Granny Simpson. 'It's a steep bank isn't it?'

'You hang onto me, Mother, and we'll be there in no time.' Bert took his mother's arm.

Edna spied a few folk from church heading towards the hospital entrance and nodded when they caught her eye. Their catholic school had been hit hard in the past couple of weeks and Sid had been the one to take it in there so she felt a bit embarrassed. Not that it had been Sid's fault. That Bevin boy had brought it here not her Sid.

They reached the main door and were about to go along the corridor that led to a large window where they could look into the boy's ward when a young nurse stopped them. 'Mr and Mrs Simpson can you come this way? Matron would like a word in her office.'

Edna's knees almost gave way. 'Is he? Is he…?'

'No, no, no,' the nurse shook her head. 'Don't think the worst, Mrs. Simpson. It's not for me to say but Matron will explain.'

Granny Simpson hung onto Bert looking grey. 'My mother's legs aren't so good could she wait here?' Bert asked.

'Certainly.' The nurse led Granny to an alcove in the corridor. You wait here and I'll send someone with a chair for you to sit on until your son collects you. Don't worry you'll look in on Sidney before you go.'

'I can see him?' The colour returned to her mother-in-law's cheeks and Edna let out a sigh. They could look in on Sidney she'd said. Edna took a deep breath. They could see him so he must be hanging in there.

Hanging in he was. When they'd talked to Matron, collected Granny Simpson and looked in on Sid through the window of his side room they could tell he was proper poorly. The nurse who had accompanied them all this time reassured them that he was critical but steady. Whatever that meant. His neck was swollen bigger than his face poor bairn.

'Is he choking? Is he being strangled by it? Granny Simpson dared to ask.

Nurse Tweedie took her hand. She pulled no punches. 'Unfortunately diphtheria patients are in danger of choking. The bacteria has caused a grey membrane to form over the back of Sid's throat. We can't remove it and it has blocked his airway. The tube the doctor has inserted in his throat is enabling him to take in some air. His body has to fight for oxygen and we can only keep him comfortable and watch and wait.'

'What are his chances, nurse?' Bert sounded as if he was holding back tears and Edna squeezed his arm.

'I'd say that his chances are the same as they are for everyone who falls this ill and we have to keep him comfortable and wait.'

'How many make it? Please be honest,' Edna asked.

'When their throat is closed like this, I'd say half pull through.' Edna recalled that matron had already told them this but they were in shock.

'Fifty fifty.' Bert nodded. 'My lad will pull through. He's a fighter.'

Nurse Tweedie said, 'I must leave you now to change into a gown then I'll go in to Sid. Are there any other questions before I go?'

Granny Simpson looked at the nurse closely. 'Are you the nurse who talked to my lodger through the window during the week?'

'I am,' Nurse Tweedie smiled. 'Your lodger shouldn't have been here but I'm sure it put you at rest to know that Sid was being well cared for. You mustn't send him again, though. It's against our rules and Matron would be furious.'

Granny Simpson nodded. 'He said you were a bonny lass and pleasant natured, and he was right.'

Edna took her mother-in law's arm and led her away. So she'd sent the other Bevin boy to look through the window? And now she was passing on comments that the lad had made. You couldn't take Granny Simpson anywhere without her showing you up.

As they were heading for the bus stop, the Fletchers passed by in their car. Edna had heard from Mary along the row that their lad was in the hospital. Having a car made the trip easier. The car pulled in just before the bus stop and Mr Fletcher, the under-manager got out.

'Good afternoon, Bert. How is your lad?' he asked.

'Not doing so well Mr Fletcher. He's in a side ward and proper poorly.'

'Sorry to hear that. It's the same for Douglas. They moved him to a side room during the week and he's struggling. Look, I've room in the back for two. Can I give the ladies a lift back?'

Oh no! Edna didn't want to make polite conversation to those two all the way home but she heard Bert saying, 'That's kind of you, my mother's legs aren't so good.'

There was nothing for it but to get in and hope Granny Simpson didn't say anything to show her up even more.

Edna was surprised that Mrs Fletcher was chatty and shared the same worries as herself. They took Granny all the way to her door at Burnside and then dropped her at the rows. He might be management but he was a kind man was Mr Fletcher, and his wife, Dorothy she insisted she call her, she was nicer than she had expected. It just goes to show that you should always accept a hand of friendship when it's offered. She'd light a candle for Douglas as well as Sid and Rose when she went church tomorrow.

8

After the visitors dispersed, Helen sponged down Sid and thought about his father's words. 'He's a fighter,' Mr Simpson had said but Helen knew that they all were. Being a fighter had nothing to do with recovery. It was all down to whether your lungs and heart and immune system were strong enough. Many a brave fighter had passed away on this ward and it just broke her heart.

When she first started at this hospital, she had shadowed another nurse. 'Sitting with Nelly' the sister called it because you followed everything an experienced nurse, a Nelly, did for several shifts until you knew all of the duties for that ward. Her Nelly had been on the isolation wards for years and had warned her not to get too involved with the families or individual patients or she would burn out and the grief would be too much. Helen tried, she really did but when you were tending sick children it was hard not to get involved. Maybe she would burn out but she couldn't stay detached.

'Come on Sid, let's make you comfy,' she whispered as the child moaned and fretted and seemed restless. She was loath to leave him but she had other patients waiting.

Her next charge was Douglas. He'd moved into a side ward earlier in the week and his parents were distraught when they found out but had every faith in the nurses.

His mother had confessed to feeling guilty about not

heeding the first signs he was ill and not knowing who he'd been playing with. Helen hoped her reassurance that so many parents felt guilty for no good reason helped to ease Mrs Fletcher's feeling of blame.

She was met with this guilt so often. Were they to blame for taking them out? Were they to blame for getting caught in the rain? Why hadn't they noticed this or that? The poor parents picked over everything that had happened before the infection but the truth was that diphtheria spread like wildfire once it got into a community and would cause its havoc whatever the community did to try to prevent it.

At the end of her shift, Helen removed her barrier nursing overall, thoroughly washed her hands and drew her outdoor cloak around her. It would be chilly and she'd be glad of its warmth for the short walk through the grounds to the nurses' quarters.

She set off walking briskly, thinking of the pot of tea waiting for her with maybe a crumpet or two. Someone else fell into step with her.

'Good evening, nurse.'

Helen knew who he was immediately; the lodger. The man who had come to see Sidney Simpson. 'What are you doing here at this time? Visiting is over.'

'Granny Simpson told me you'd been really helpful this afternoon and you were on duty so I thought I'd catch the bus and come along.' He had a pleasant voice and a lovely smile.

'Why? Why have you come along?' Was it just to see her? She wondered.

'To see you.'

'To see me?'

'Yes to see you and to ask you out. To ask you to the pictures. Would you like to come with me tonight or one evening through the week?'

They were almost at the nurses' quarters. Helen wasn't sure what to say.

She stopped at the steps to her quarters and there was a moment's silence as they both looked at one another.

'I'm sorry. I don't know you and my work keeps me busy,' she answered at last.

'I'd like us to get to know each other. We could go for a short walk tomorrow and you could get to know me a bit better.'

She was off duty tomorrow but should she? 'Can I think about it?' Helen asked.

'Yes of course. If you decide you want to take a walk, I'll meet you at the main gates tomorrow at say three o'clock?'

'Okay I'll think about it and maybe I'll see you then.'

Helen went inside her quarters with flushed cheeks and it wasn't just the crisp winter air. Did she have a date? Should she go? She'd make her tea and crumpets in the kitchen first and then discuss her offer with her friends in the common room.

It had been unanimous. They'd asked what he looked like and what he did. She didn't know why he was in the area but she could describe his sparkling blue eyes and dark wavy hair and his deep voice. The common room committee had decided that she should take the walk and then decide on whether to go out to the pictures another time. What was the harm in a Sunday stroll?

So here she was and he wasn't here. Helen kicked at the dry leaves by the gate and was about to turn back when a bus pulled up. Matt jumped off and ran up to her. 'I'm so sorry. Sunday service and the buses aren't so frequent,' he said breathlessly.

'Keeping a lady waiting.' Helen shook her head.

'Please accept my apology and these.' He pulled a packet of sweets from his pocket.

'What are they?' Helen peeked into the packet.

'I thought we could share some chocolate eclairs,' he said.

'One of my favourites,' Helen laughed and the ice was broken.

They set off for a walk in the woods by the grounds and were soon sharing the sweets and chatting like old friends.

'What made you take up nursing?' Matt asked as they stopped for a rest on a tree trunk and watched by the fast flowing burn on its way to join the River Tyne.

'I've always wanted to nurse and I've enjoyed every placement especially this one, it's the hardest but my favourite,' Helen confided. 'Seeing children recover and go home is just wonderful but there's the other side, the young lives we couldn't save and it's hard some weeks.'

'I don't know how you do it but I'm glad there are people like you to make little nippers' lives easier. It's worthwhile. I wanted to join the army and do something worthwhile but it wasn't to be.' He skilfully skimmed a stone so it jumped across the fast-flowing water.

'I wondered why you weren't in the forces. If you wanted to join up you mustn't be a Connie. Are you excused on medical grounds?' The tell-tale twitch in his cheek told Helen she had touched a nerve.

'No I'm fit as you can see and more than ready to fight. Lots of people think I'm a Connie but the truth is I was unlucky. I was one of the unlucky blighters to be drawn out of the conscription hat and assigned to travel north to the pits. Ernest Bevin's idea to keep the mines going.' His rueful smile showed his regret at being here instead of fighting abroad.

'Miners are playing their part too. We need fuel as much as we need soldiers and nurses. You should be proud of playing the part you've been given.' Helen took his arm and they stood up to walk back towards her home.

'I feel more lucky today, walking here and chatting to you. I'm an outdoor person and my family are farmers.'

'Really? My dad is a blacksmith for the farms around Rothbury and I think you'd like it around there. It's hilly with sheep and cattle farming more than arable. My brother followed him into the trade but he's in the army so Dad has to work on his own.'

'I miss fresh air more than anything when I'm mining. On our farm, we have the WLA's land girls helping out so joining the army seemed the best option and would've made my dad proud. He was in the First World War.'

'He's not proud of you doing this?' Helen asked.

'He's furious. Not with me but with the government for sending me underground.'

'You'll go back to farming?'

'When the war's over. I'm skilled at growing crops and mending machinery and here, I'm a novice. I'd be okay with the pit machinery, fixing it and stuff but once you get to the mine, the miners don't trust you to know anything. It's frustrating. To top it all, Ron, my fellow lodger, brought diphtheria to Burnside and we're all even less popular.'

'Are they sure it was him?'

'Oh yes, he went home to a wedding and there had been a few cases around the area. They think that's how Sid caught it and why Granny Simpson feels so bad about it.'

'My understanding is that there is an outbreak as near as Durham and the trains going south stop there. There's no way of being sure where you get it because it takes a while to incubate and some carriers don't even have symptoms.'

'I'll tell Mrs Simpson that.' Matt took Helen's hand to help her over a rough piece of track. 'It's been great to be out in the fresh air and talk to a friendly face. Could we do it again next weekend?'

'I'm sorry Matt, I'm working next Sunday.'

'I suppose you wouldn't come to the pictures with me next Saturday night?' The words rushed out and he squeezed the hand he was still holding onto.

What could she say? 'As long as I pick the film and you stop crushing my hand.'

Matt rewarded her with a dazzling smile and linked her arm to walk her back towards the nurses' quarters.

9

Ginnie had bought the cream wool for Rose's Christmas cardigan. David had the hank of wool looped over his wrists with his arms apart while she unwound the hank and rolled it into manageable balls of wool.

'Mam, my arms are aching,' he complained.

'Stanley come and take over from your brother,' she called.

'It's sissy's work that, Mam. Do I have to?'

'What would Father Christmas say if he could hear your grumbles?' It was three weeks to Christmas so the old man's visit was being used all around the rows to cajole bairns to behave.

Stanley took over and she carried on rolling the wool. She was working it in with the spare blue wool to make a patterned cardigan for Rose. There was no need to hide the knitting now because they'd been told that Rose wouldn't be home until after Christmas. The cardigan would be waiting for her when she got home. Gifts to the hospital had to be food or something that would be left there because of infection.

She was still awful poorly but on the main ward for girls. John had gone on his own to see her, well to stand by the window and look in on her on Saturday.

Ginnie had tossed and turned and fretted for nights about whether to try to go or not. Would she be able to get her foot through the door? Would her fear of hospitals hold her back?

In the end, John hadn't even asked her. On Saturday morning he'd said, 'Why don't you make a few girdle scones for me to take to the hospital with a jar of your rhubarb jam? The nurses or the bairns who are well enough will enjoy them. I'll go to the hospital whilst you look after the twins because there's no need for both of us to spend the bus fare just to look through a window.'

He'd let her off the hook. He knew her too well. She'd agreed gladly but it hadn't sat well with her all weekend. She so wanted to see Rose. She wanted to know what the hospital was like but she couldn't control her breathing or stop her hands from trembling when she thought of the place. Maybe next weekend?

Edna Simpson was sitting in her Sunday best with Mary-from-next-door on Sunday night when Ginnie called with one of the fresh teacakes she'd made that afternoon.

'Hello Ginnie, I've just got off the bus from church and thought I'd have a few minutes with Mary before I face the Sunday night chores. I've persuaded Eileen to get the others into their night clothes.'

The catholic church was in the next village and Edna would have been lighting a candle for Sid.

'How is he doing Edna?' she asked as Mary handed her a strong black tea from the pot.

'Not well at all, Ginnie. We can just pray for the poor bairns and hope God's angels are a match for that bad 'un in our midst. I lit a candle for your Rose and for Douglas Fletcher too. He's struggling.' She sipped her tea. 'We saw John on the bus to the hospital yesterday. How's Rose?'

Edna probably meant no harm but Ginnie's guilt at not going caused her face to flush and her heart raced. 'She's not great. I couldn't leave the boys yesterday but I'll go next time.' Ginnie wished she could gulp her tea and go.

'I'm sorry I let you down, pet, but I had my hands full with him upstairs and couldn't watch the twins. Ever so poorly he was.' Mary patted Ginnie's shoulder.

Ginnie breathed a sigh. Mary was backing her up. She hadn't asked Mary to watch the bairns but Edna knew that Mary would always oblige with child minding. 'Thanks Mary,' was all she could say.

Mary and Tom had been the best of neighbours. Having the roomy end-of-terrace outhouse, Ginnie shared washing days with Mary and she was like the mother she didn't have. Tom was ill with the black lung, his legacy for working amongst pit dust for forty years, and had good days and bad so Edna would believe Mary's story.

'I must go now,' Ginnie carried her cup into the scullery. 'I need to get the twins bathed and ready for school tomorrow. I'll be glad when it closes for Christmas and then maybe the strangling angel will leave its corridors and fly elsewhere.'

'Yes, I'd better get back to my lot too,' Edna stood up to leave. 'I'll be back at church on Friday. It's our feast of the immaculate conception so I'll light another candle for Rose.'

'Thanks,' Ginnie was grateful but couldn't help feeling irritated. Did Edna think she had a much better line to God's ear than the rest of them?

Mary took a coin from her pinny and pushed it into Edna's hand. 'Here pet. Light two,' she said, giving Ginnie a wink. She saw them to the back door. 'I'll be around to start washing at nine once they're away to school, Ginnie.'

Ginnie called, 'Yes I'll get the boiler going and the kettle on.'

10

Helen had worked an extra tough shift last night. It was a blustery day and the clouds sped across the grey December sky as she sat by the window of the communal kitchen and sipped her tea. The window was draughty and she wrapped her dressing gown tightly around her.

She didn't feel like meeting Matt. They were both working night shifts so they'd made an arrangement to go to the Coliseum in Morpeth to see *It's in the Bag*, a comedy. She liked Matt and it would be nice to see a film but she couldn't shake off that nightmare of a shift.

She had fallen into bed at eight o'clock that morning and tossed and turned for hours before falling asleep. Her sleep had been restless and dream filled and her first thought on waking had been that poor lad. They'd spent the night fighting to keep him and, in the early hours, they'd lost him. The doctor said it was his heart in the end.

It always hit her hard. Not so long ago, diphtheria had killed half of its victims until its antitoxin came along, an antitoxin that worked wonders on most. There were still some who didn't respond or had complications and the hospital statistics showed one in ten didn't make it.

Helen hated it. There was the helpless feeling of watching a child struggle for breath, the sadness as that young life slipped away and then the pain of having to inform the parents. Every time, she wondered whether she was cut out to be a nurse. Every time, she had to accept that the pain went with the joy of seeing other children get well.

With a sigh, she stood up and washed her cup out. She may as well get dressed and meet Matt. If she stayed here and stood him up, it wouldn't be fair to him and she would just sit and brood until her next shift came around. That poor lad though, his life had hardly begun. People were shocked when they discovered how many children had died in this war through bomb attacks but the medical figures showed that even more were dying from diphtheria.

She was a minute or two late but Matt was standing under the Coliseum's sign and his eyes lit up as she approached. Helen mustered a smile and put work firmly to the back of her mind. She wouldn't taint the afternoon by talking about her woes, this was a short reprieve.

The film, about two batty sisters who tried to track down a dress that had a fortune sewn in the hem, was just what Helen needed to take her mind away from that sick room. She shared a bag of Butterkist popcorn with Matt and he took her hand in his during the last part of the film. She found herself imagining what it would be like if he leaned over and kissed her. Would she mind? No. She glanced at his profile, he had well-shaped lips, and she imagined them on hers.

After the film, they headed to a nearby café around the corner. They were sitting with a pot of tea, waiting for their fish and chips with bread and spread to arrive. 'Fish and chips will set me up nicely for my shift,' Matt said. 'Down the pit, I just take a bit of bait and a can of cold tea to wash down the dust.'

'A bit of bait? You sound like you're off fishing.' Helen poured the tea.

'The miner's around here call the food they take to work their bait. Mrs Simpson makes me two rounds of jam and marg every day and I'm ready for it after a few hours of putting.'

'What is that?'

'I'm a putter. I move the full tubs of coal to the pit eye, that's the bottom where the cage is, and then I take empty tubs to the coal face for filling. It's heavy work and you have to keep on your toes but I'm lucky to be doing that because a lot of the Bevin boys are kept up top to pick over the coal and that's no fun. At least my shift goes quickly. I'm getting used to the dialect of the men I work with; their crack is funny at bait time.'

'You're starting to fit in then? You said it was hard being the new man.'

'I fit in as long as I keep my head down and don't get above my station in the pit's hierarchy. I listen and I laugh but I keep my mouth shut. I've found that's best.'

Helen realised that she wasn't the only one with a difficult job, Matt must find it hard living here away from family and friends.

'Are you going home for Christmas?' It wasn't far off and Helen was crossing the days off on her calendar.

'I'd like to but I daren't. It would worry Mrs Simpson and it might cause a stir along the row. Ever since Ron came back with diphtheria, they've hinted that I'd better not go back home and bring more germs here. I think it's best if I stay with the Simpsons this year, though I'll feel like a spare part. Will Sidney get out for Christmas?'

'Little Sidney? Yes he's on the mend at last, he's on the main ward now and likely to be discharged just before.'

'I'm glad to hear that. Can I tell Granny Simpson?'

'It might be best to let Sid's parents find out first on their Saturday visit.'

'Okay, my lips are sealed.'

Helen wondered when he would seal his lips on hers. She

had only kissed one other boy and it hadn't been anything to shout about but, when she looked at Matt, she imagined kissing him would be different altogether.

They tucked into their fish and chips and an idea came to Helen. Should she ask? Her parents wouldn't mind. In fact, they'd certainly be interested in seeing who was courting their daughter.

'Matt, if you're not going back home, you might want to come with me to meet my parents and my brother's wife and family on Christmas day? It's not so far to travel.' She felt her cheeks flush.

'Would they have me? Would they want a stranger? They know nothing about me.'

'I'll tell them about you. I'll write and say you're coming. I finish work on Saturday so I'm setting off on Sunday morning, Christmas Eve, and coming back on Boxing Day. You'd have to stay over too because there is no transport running on Christmas Day.'

'Spend Christmas with you? I'd love that, Helen, but is there room?'

'You could have my brother's old room, he slept above the forge before he got married. It's basic but you're welcome, that is if you want to. Do you?' Her tummy fluttered, was it with nerves or excitement?

'Sleep above a forge in the countryside and get away from that pit wheel looming above the rows? Have more time to be with you? What do you think, Helen?' He beamed at her.

She'd love it too. Matt had turned today, a dreadful day, into something a bit more bearable. She really liked him, liked him a lot and hoped her parents would too.

ll

Dorothy picked up the phone on the second ring. 'Linwood 289'

'Good afternoon Mrs. Fletcher. It's Matron's assistant. I'm ringing to see if you could come in to see her today.'

'Douglas? Is he alright? I mean, he's no worse is he?' she gripped the phone and her hand shook so much it was clattering onto her earring. She pulled the earring off saying, 'Is there news?'

'I'm sorry Mrs Simpson, I've just been asked to invite you into the hospital today. Matron would like to see you. I can't give you any more details.'

Can't or won't thought Dorothy. Heart pounding, she said, 'We'll come in as soon as possible. I'll get in touch with my husband now.'

This wasn't good. This wasn't good at all. On Monday, they'd been called by the hospital suggesting they go to see Douglas because he had deteriorated. Matron had met them and told them it was touch and go so they could sit awhile with him but had to remain outside of his room.

The corridor was quiet and two chairs were waiting for them by the large window. Douglas's bed had been pulled right over to the window and they could see how he was labouring to get his breath. Dorothy laboured with every breath too and willed him to pull through. Eventually, a nurse had tapped her shoulder and gently said it was time for them to leave.

'I can't leave him struggling like this alone.' Dorothy broke down in tears.

The nurse hugged her and promised she would sit by him all night. 'He won't be alone Mrs Fletcher. I'll make sure he's comfortable and do all I can for him.'

'Will he get better?' she pleaded.

'That's not for any of us to know or guess. At this stage, we can only watch and wait. You have a telephone so we can inform you if there's a change.'

'Thank you, nurse. What's your name?' Dorothy asked.

'Nurse Tweedie, Helen Tweedie,' the nurse answered.

Dorothy had gone home in a daze and sat by the telephone for the last two days.

Now this call. Was it bad news or had he come through?

She quickly dialled Neville's number at the pit head. He answered first ring. 'It's Dorothy. I've had a call. We have to go to the hospital. How soon can you leave work?'

'I'm coming now. I'll be outside in two minutes.'

Dorothy was at the door and watching for the car. The sooner they got to the hospital, the sooner they'd know how their boy was doing.

Neither of them spoke on the journey to the hospital. Like her, Neville was deep inside his own thoughts. She twisted her gloves in her hands. Douglas had been very poorly on Monday night but this was Wednesday and maybe he had come out of that crisis. Maybe the matron wanted to tell them and let them see him for themselves.

The m atron met t hem a t h er office doo r. She mus t hav e had someone watch for them arriving. 'Good afternoon Mr Fletcher, Mrs Fletcher, come inside.'

The woman was straight-faced and, after the door closed, she stood rigidly in front of them. 'Take a seat, please.'

There were three seats in front of her desk. They all took one. Matron usually sat behind her desk. Helen could hardly breathe and had the sensation that she was looking from above at three tiny figures, she wasn't in the room at all. Was she going to faint?

'How is Douglas?' Neville broke the silence.

'I'm sorry to be the bearer of bad news but I must tell you that Douglas slipped away in the early hours of the morning.'

'No! No, that can't be,' Dorothy shook her head. 'I would have known.'

'I'm afraid it's true, Mrs Fletcher. We have followed all necessary procedures and you may go to your son, shortly.'

'Can we take him home? Can we have him with us until the funeral? Neville asked.

'You may see Douglas for a short time but it will be a closed coffin afterwards and he must remain here or go to an undertakers. It's health measures, I'm sure you understand, Mr Fletcher.'

What were they talking about? Her son, her only child could not be dead. She must see him. She stood up, her legs gave way and she fell into darkness.

When Dorothy woke up, she was lying across the back seat of their car. She tried to sit up. They were travelling away from the hospital and the shock hit her for a second time. Douglas was dead. 'Neville, where are you going? I need to see him.'

Neville pulled the car to one side of the road and parked. He turned around in his seat. 'It was too much for you, Dorothy. The matron thought it best if I saw Douglas and then took you home. They called a doctor and he's given you a sedative injection to help you sleep. Please don't fight it.'

'I want to see my son. I need to see him.' She pressed her knuckles to her mouth and bit hard on them to stop her teeth from chattering. Douglas had gone and she needed to say goodbye.

'Believe me when I say that it is best you remember him as he was on Monday. You sat with him then and you have that memory. It's just his body left, Dorothy. The life has gone out of him and I wouldn't wish you to see that. I wish I hadn't.' Tears were coursing down Neville's face.

'I can't remember the last time I held him.'

Neville got out of the driver's seat and slid in beside her. He held her and rocked her. 'Hush, hush.' They clutched each other and cried for their loss, for their wonderful son who had been taken by the strangling angel's deadly kiss and Dorothy felt herself relax and fall into a thick blanket of nothing again.

12

Ginnie stood over the range checking the beef stew for to-night's dinner. She was popping it back into the oven because it needed another good half hour when John came home from his shift. He strode over to give her a hug as usual but kept tight hold and buried his head in her neck. Something was wrong. 'What is it John? Has somebody been hurt?' John was part of the pit's rescue team and was often first to arrive at a nasty scene.

He took a step back and clasped both her hands. 'No Ginnie, it's not work. It's the Fletchers' lad.'

'Has he taken a turn for the worse?' Fear swept through Ginnie. Lots of Linwood bairns were so far away and so sick and her Rose was one of them. 'What have you heard, John?'

His eyes brimmed with tears. 'They've lost him, pet. They were told yesterday and Mr Fletcher wasn't in today. The over-man told us all at lowse, before we came home. Mr Fletcher, he's management but he's fair, what a blow to the man. We were all choked for him.'

Ginnie had to sit down because of that tight feeling in her chest again, that helplessness. Poor Mrs Fletcher. She only had the one and she'd brought him up so well. He had a lot more than the bairns in the row but he was polite, he played with them without airs and graces and he never bragged. His mother would be kicking herself for sending him into school because didn't mothers always look at what they could've done differently?

Ginnie took her pinny off and hung it on the scullery door. A fresh apple pie was waiting on the bench for after their dinner and a smaller one for Mary. Mary wouldn't mind, they'd make do with the small one and she'd take the bigger one around to the Fletchers'. 'I'm calling around, just to let them know we're sorry for their loss. I won't be long, John. If the twins are hungry, give them a slice of bread to share until I get back.'

Mr Fletcher answered the door. He looked dazed.

'I've brought a pie for you and Mrs Fletcher and I've come to say how sorry we are to hear the news about your lad, Douglas.' Ginnie handed the pie to Mr Fletcher who took it and looked as if he didn't know what to do with it. 'If you put it in the larder, it will last a day or two for when you're hungry or have visitors.'

'Ah, yes. Yes, I'll do that and thank you, Mrs Kelly. I hope Rose continues to improve. Would you like to come in and sit with Dorothy? She's not been too good but company might help.'

Ginnie wasn't expecting an invitation in. She'd never crossed the door of the under-manager's large house on the edge of the colliery grounds. 'I'll pop in for a moment. I've got the dinner on but it needs another half hour in the oven.'

Mr Fletcher turned and she followed him along a hall-way into a kitchen larger than her own, with two cushioned chairs by the range. The window was framed with pretty floral curtains but it wasn't as grand as she'd feared. Mrs Fletcher was sitting at the kitchen table with her hands in her lap and gazing out of the window towards the pit yard. She turned as they entered and as Ginnie said a shy, 'Hello, Mrs Fletcher,' she heard the wobble of tears in her own voice.

'You're Rose's mother aren't you? Douglas never stopped talking about how clever Rose Kelly was. I think he had a boyish crush on your daughter.' As her clouded eyes met Ginnie's, she could see that the woman was taking some heavy medication.

'He was a fine lad. Rose and Douglas were very competitive at mental arithmetic and spelling tests,' Ginnie said. She stood wondering whether to take her leave or stay a while.

'Do sit down Mrs Kelly.' Mrs Fletcher said before turning to her husband. 'Neville, could you bring Mrs Kelly and me a glass of sherry each and then maybe you could leave us to have a chat?'

Ginnie wasn't expecting this to be a social call but she took the chair opposite Mrs Fletcher. Sherry before dinner, and through the week? This wasn't a good way for Mrs Fletcher to go on.

'I feel numb, Mrs Kelly. Just numb. I can't quite believe our news.'

'Call me Ginnie, please,'

'Then you must call me Dorothy. Dot, my friends at school called me but I hated being a Dot. What's Ginnie shortened from?'

'Virginia after my grandmother. Quite a mouthful so I prefer Ginnie.'

'I didn't want Douglas to be shortened to Doug but he was called Dougie by the boys in the school yard and he loved it.'

They sipped sherry and chatted about names and children as if they were just passing the time of day.

'It's time I left. I am sorry for your loss, Dorothy. If there's anything I can do…' Ginnie stood up.

Dorothy stood to see her out and her eyes cleared for a moment. 'It hasn't hit me yet but I know it's coming. I have tablets and as they are wearing off I take a sherry but I know the time will come when I have to go up those stairs and into his room and face the unbearable. He's never coming back is he?'

Ginnie took Dorothy in her arms and hugged her. Never mind manners or convention, words weren't comfort enough. She withdrew and wiped tears from her own eyes but Dorothy stood dazed and dry eyed. 'You are very kind. Thanks for calling and please come again. I don't know what I'll do with my days now. Now that...' She stopped and slumped back onto her chair.

'I will call again, take care.' Ginnie walked along the hallway and let herself out.

She hurried along to her own row. She was lucky to have her boys and John waiting for her. She felt determined too. She was going to conquer her silly fear and go to see her daughter this weekend.

Her courage had wavered by Saturday. Ginnie was silent all the way to the bus stop and couldn't engage in conversation with the other visitors who boarded the bus. There were only two Saturday visits before Christmas and the bus was full of the relatives of sick children. They could take what they wanted but nothing would return home so most of the visitors settled for fruit and food treats.

Ginnie had been given a pile of old books from Miss Wakenshaw who had assured her she was finished with them and they could remain at the hospital. Rose would be delighted. She couldn't wait to see her face but she had to get through the doors first.

They walked up to the huge main entrance doors with a gaggle of other parents, John holding tightly to her arm. 'Are you ready for this, Ginnie?' he asked.

With a quick, 'No!' she pulled away from him and dashed around a large bush to be sick. She heaved but thankfully she didn't throw up.

John joined her and rubbed her back. 'Rose can't see you like this, Ginnie. You've tried your best but I can see you're not going to get past those doors today. You wait outside on the bench under that tree and I'll go in myself.'

'I so wanted to see her, John but I can't bring myself to climb those steps.' She searched his eyes to see if he understood.

'Here give me the bag of books and you sit quietly until I come back. I'll tell Rose you're just outside and you tried. She'll understand.'

Ginnie watched his back as he walked towards the dreaded doors. What a failure she was. What a hopeless mother.

She felt better sitting under the tree. It was chilly but a bright day for the time of year and, after a while, a robin made an appearance on the branch of a nearby shrub. She was so entranced that it startled her when someone sat beside her.

'Are you watching Rascal, our resident robin? I've come along early before my shift just to spot him because he cheers me up.' The pretty woman with blonde curly hair wore a nurse's cloak. She took a paper bag from inside her cloak and sprinkled crumbs in front of them.

'Yes, I've been watching his antics. I'm waiting for my husband to come and collect me but he'll be a while. He's visiting.'

'Have you already been in?' The nurse sprinkled more crumbs.

'No I… I can't. I can't get myself near to the building. I've such a fear of hospitals, you see.' She gabbled on, 'It's daft I know, but I can't help myself.'

The nurse toughed her arm gently. 'It's not daft at all. I have a fear of heights but luckily I can avoid them most of the time.'

'I've avoided hospitals all of my life but now my daughter is in there. What I'd give to cross the threshold to see her. Do you know her, Rose Kelly? I'm Ginnie Kelly.'

'I'm Helen, Nurse Tweedie when I'm on duty. Where exactly is she?'

'The main diphtheria ward.'

The cheeky robin hopped right by their feet to take the nurse's last offerings. She stood up saying, 'Follow me. I think I've got the answer.'

'I can't go in there.' Ginnie remained seated

'No need to go inside. Come with me and I'll show you the outside window to the girls' ward.'

Ginnie followed and Nurse Tweedie pointed to the window. She pulled a crate from the shrubbery 'See this crate? It's used by the parents who sneak a mid-week peek. Put it back when you leave. I must go to my own ward now. I'm on duty in the boys' end after visiting.'

'Thank you, nurse.'

'Careful you don't slip or I'll be in trouble.'

Ginnie stepped onto the crate and had a clear view of the ward. Her heart pounded at the sight of rows of beds and nurses dressed in long white aprons moving but she took a deep breath and didn't turn away. Eventually, her head cleared enough for her to pick out Rose. She was at the far end of the ward at another window. That would be the window from the corridor and she would be talking to John.

Ginnie took in the layout of the ward. A large table with chairs at one end, that would be where they would eat, if they were well. A book case and a few toys on a shelf and a black board and easel sat in one corner. The beds were narrow and in tidy rows. Which was Rose's? She spotted one nearby with a book lying open on the bed. That might be hers.

It was all as clinical as she imagined but she was not fearful of it now that she was here and looking in. Rose was walking away from the window and towards the bed, the one with the book on it. She picked up the book and stopped. She paused as if she could sense someone watching her.

Ginnie dared to give a little tap on the window and Rose swung around. Her eyes widened as she saw her. 'Mam!' She rushed to the window and tears poured down Ginnie's cheeks. Her girl was pale and thinner with dark circles under her eyes but when she came nearer her eyes were bright and she looked like she was on the mend.

'Rose. Hello my sweetheart. I couldn't step into the building but I've found you.'

'Dad told me you were being a scaredy cat. Fancy being frightened of a hospital. Really Mam, at your age. The nurses are making me well and I'll be home soon.'

'I can see that pet.'

'I won't be home for Christmas though. Can you imagine being stuck here? I'll miss your Christmas dinner.'

'We'll keep your presents for when you get home but I'll try to come again before then. I'll come next Saturday and if I'm still a scaredy cat then I'll be at this window.'

'Righty-ho Mam. Give my love to the twins and tell Lottie I'm getting better. How's Sid? How's Douglas? Dad forgot to say.'

'I have to go to meet your dad, pet. I'll see you next week.' Ginnie stepped down and hurried back to the seat to meet John. Rose didn't need to hear the sad news about Douglas yet.

13

On Saturday, Edna allowed Eileen and Lottie to visit the isolation hospital with Bert and Granny Simpson and she stayed home. Sidney would love seeing his sisters and she had far too much to do before Christmas. She'd let her housework go all to pot over the past few weeks and pit dust was quick to slip into the house when you weren't looking. Sidney was coming home for Christmas so it was high time she tackled the dust and put a shine on the house again.

Christmas was a Monday this year and the ambulance would bring Sid back on the Friday before. She wanted to spring clean their main bedroom even though it had been done in spring. Alfie and Sidney shared a bed built in the alcove of the main bedroom with a curtain pulled across. It was a squash at the best of times but what could they do with two bedrooms and four bairns?

Before she set about with a collection of cleaning rags, carbolic, bicarbonate of soda and a scrubbing brush, she was getting the chimney swept so they could light a bedroom fire for a day or two, just until Sid was used to being back home and in a chillier bedroom. Edna wanted no setbacks and they had plenty of coal in the shed. Bert liked to sell a barrow or two if he could but he'd not be doing that this quarter because the extra coal was going to keep the two bairns warm in their bed.

Alfie had been given the job of sorting out their comics and marbles from under the bed and then she'd give him a list of groceries to take to Norris's shop. They weren't letting the bairns roam far just yet, so she was keeping him close by.

Edna wanted to use today as a baking day and a day to wrap presents before she had a full house again. She was so looking forward to having all her family under one roof for Christmas.

Poor Mrs Fletcher, her life would never be the same. The funeral was on Thursday and, although it was in the Methodist chapel, she would go. She was just thankful that Sidney had come through none the worse.

She made a clootie fruit pudding with apples from the allotment and a small handful of dried fruit. Alfie yammered for a handful and she thought, why not? He was never any bother and he loved his food.

They would have bacon and cabbage with taties then the pudding with custard. It was hard to manage on a pitman's wages and rationing made it even more of a struggle but they had their allotment and she was a dab hand at cooking so the Simpsons never starved.

Once Alfie had been sent to the shops and told to call to see if Mary wanted anything, Edna took her stack from the back of her dresser. She had new nighties for the girls and a proper bottle of Drene shampoo for them to share.

There was a jigsaw for Sidney and an annual for Alfie and she had knitted them both black and white balaclavas. By unravelling a pair of old black socks and an old baby's matinee set that she wouldn't use any more, she had come up with enough wool for a Magpies striped hat each. They looked grand. Make do and mend and reusing old wool had been a skill in these rows long before the war made it popular.

Bert would get a holey old pit stocking filled with a large potato and a carrot before he found his pouch of baccie at the toe, and that would make the bairns laugh.

Christmas had its traditions and Edna loved this season. She hummed 'Adeste Fideles' as she wrapped the presents in brown paper, labelled them, then tied them up with scraps of ribbon kept in her sewing box especially for presents. They'd be put away and kept to use again next year and the year after.

She had just hidden the wrapped gifts away when the door opened and Lottie and Eileen came in with Bert and were quickly followed by Alfie dragging the shopping bag. Edna felt blessed and couldn't wait for Sidney, her other little lamb, to be back in the fold.

Dinner was finished, every plate was clean and Edna was just about to cut into the pudding when it started; Wailing Willie. 'Not tonight! They had all had a lovely day and now they were going to spend the next few hours in the cold Anderson shelter, across the row in their allotment. 'Lottie you grab the custard, Eileen take the dishes and spoons, Bert take the teapot, it's just brewed, Alfie bring my knitting bag, I've got the pudding.'

In no time they were packed into the shelter and Edna was dishing out the afters. Hitler and his henchmen might be targeting Tyne docks but their threat of V-1 flying bombs, those noisy doodlebugs, weren't spoiling their Saturday treat.

14

It was a bright sunny but bitterly cold day when Helen set off for Linwood. She had swapped her nurse's duty to go to Douglas Fletcher's funeral. Whenever possible, she attended the funerals of the children she had nursed because it gave her some sort of closure and she needed that. Matt offered to go along with her because he lodged in the next village. He would meet her off the bus and they'd find the chapel together.

Matt had been assured by Granny Simpson that there was even less at Linwood than there was in Burnside. 'That's hard to imagine, Helen,' he'd told her last Sunday as they took a brisk winter walk by the fast-flowing burn near her quarters. 'Burnside has fifteen rows of houses, a couple of pubs, a village hall where they hold their dances and other activities, a church, a school and a row of shops so don't blink or you'll pass by Linwood's bus stop.'

Helen laughed. 'I've a tongue in my head. I'll ask the driver to make sure he stops at Linwood.'

Today they found out Granny Simpson hadn't exaggerated. Linwood serviced its colliery and nothing else. The Methodist chapel wasn't hard to find because it stood next to the school and opposite the working men's institute. The tallest landmarks were the pit wheel and the slag heap that towered over five rows of colliery houses.

Helen took in the view of industry mingling with countryside. Linwood nestled in a dale surrounded by farmland and patchwork carpet of allotments sat behind the five rows of colliery houses that led up to the pit head. Dark green fells could be seen rising behind the pit wheel and the railway line that transported coal from the pit was flanked at either side by hedges that looked bare now that they had shed their leaves. Even in winter, it was a greener place than Helen had imagined.

A hearse and another dark car stood outside a large house to the side of the mine. A couple of men dressed in black were standing beside the cars. 'That must be the lad's house,' Matt whispered.

'Yes, his father is the under-manager. They'll be leaving from the house at two o'clock.'

Helen and Matt reached the Methodist church with its main doors wide open and the place so packed that some of the men were standing at the back. Granny Simpson waved them over, 'I've managed to keep one seat. Your lass can sit with me and you stand at the back with the men, Matt.'

Helen slid into the place that was offered. His lass? She stifled a grin. She'd never been somebody's lass before.

Ginnie was just about to walk over to the Methodist chapel when there was a knock and Danny Dodd from Third Row was standing in her back yard. 'I've been sent with a note from Mr Fletcher. He's asked me to make sure it gets into your hands only.'

Ginnie took the note and the lad ran off. She skimmed through it.

John called from the bedroom, 'Who is that at the door, Ginnie? Can you help me with my tie? I'm all fingers and thumbs and it won't sit right.'

'Ask Mary-from-next-door to help you. You'll have to take the twins there for me anyway because I have to go to see Mrs Fletcher.'

'Mrs Fletcher?' John came down with his tie loose and looking flustered.

'Yes John. I've just had a note to say she's in a state and won't get into the funeral car. Mr Fletcher wants me to sit with her.'

'You go, pet. Has she no family with her, the poor lass? I'll see to the twins.'

When Ginnie arrived at the Fletchers', the undertaker was standing by the hearse, his teenage son was dressed in black and standing in front of it ready to lead the procession. Mr Fletcher was pacing up and down, an elderly couple, grandparents most likely, were already in the second car. A few folk from Fifth Row were looking from their doorways. You'd think if they weren't at the funeral, they'd stay inside.

Mr Fletcher rushed towards her, beads of sweat on his brow. 'Thank goodness you came promptly, Mrs Kelly. Look after Dorothy, please. We're late and I must go but I hate to leave her. Sit with her until we return.'

With a nod, Ginnie entered the house and closed the door behind her. She leaned against the door and took a breath before heading for the kitchen.

The kitchen table was heavily laden with sandwiches, cakes and pastries covered in clean white tea towels. They'd got caterers in to do all this. Cups and saucers and tea plates were stacked on the sideboard in readiness for guests after the service. Dorothy wasn't there.

She stepped into the hallway and called, 'Dorothy?' Silence. Opening the door on the opposite side of the hallway, she peered into a nicely furnished parlour. No Dorothy. The next room was small with a desk and chair, and the smell of leather mingled with tobacco filled the room. Mr Fletcher's study was empty.

'Dorothy are you upstairs?' She called.

A sniff and a quiet, 'Yes I'm up here. I see they've gone,' came from an upstairs room.

Ginnie climbed the stairs and found Dorothy standing by the window facing the street. The room was Douglas's, she knew that in an instant by the toys and games and the cricket bat by the bed. 'May I come in?'

Dorothy turned and a shadow of a smile flitted across her face. 'Yes, of course. I'm glad Neville sent for you. He was at his wit's end but I couldn't, I just couldn't follow that coffin. I've said my goodbyes in here, you see, and I don't want to hear a sermon or uplifting hymns. I'm just too angry with God right now. Can you understand that?' Dorothy sat on the bed.

'I think I can, pet.' Ginnie loosened her coat.

'Take off your coat and stay awhile, please.'

Ginnie took off her coat, lay it over a chair and sat next to Dorothy.

'Can we stay here in Douglas's room?' Dorothy asked. 'I'm perfectly happy to face the fuss of them all afterwards. I'll serve them tea and cakes when it's over.'

Dorothy didn't look quite right. She had a glazed look to her eyes and it seemed to Ginnie that she had been on too much medication. 'I can sympathise with you getting the bit between your teeth and refusing to go to the funeral. I can't set foot in a hospital. No amount of persuading can get me through those doors.'

'Why is that?' Dorothy asked.

'It harks back to my mother, I think. I know how angry a sudden death can make you because of her. I lost my mother when I was a little lassie and I'm still angry about that now.'

'Tell me how you coped. Tell me I'll get over this,' Dorothy closed her eyes as though she was only half present.

Ginnie talked and Dorothy lay back on Douglas's pillow

and listened. They sat for a long time in silence and Ginnie thought Dorothy was asleep. A welcome escape from this sorry day.

Edna arrived early at the Methodist chapel with Lottie and Eileen, Bert was coming along later to stand at the back and Mary along the row was watching over Alfie with the Kelly twins. She adjusted the scarf covering her head feeling strange about entering a different place of worship.

The chapel seemed plain compared to her own church but it had the cross at the front. There was no advent wreath to be seen and there were festive jars of holly and Christmas roses on the sills. She clenched her rosary in her coat pocket, she wouldn't get it out but it comforted her being there. She knew in her head it was the same lord they were praying to but her heart said that he preferred her catholic church's ways.

Oh but it was a lovely service, she had to admit. 'All Things Bright and Beautiful' to bring the coffin in. A talk about the lad from his headmaster and then a poem read by another teacher. That Miss Wakenshaw, in her clear voice, read a poem about death being nothing at all and him just being in another room.

There wasn't a dry eye when Miss Wakenshaw led the children in Douglas's Sunday school class into singing 'Jesus Bids Us Shine'. They all placed candles around the coffin as they sang.

That's when she felt the love in the chapel wrap itself around her and she let go of her grip on her rosary. This was a different house of God but it gave her the same feeling as her own.

They left the chapel to bury Douglas in the little cemetery between Linwood and Burnside and she noticed Mr Fletcher was on his own with two elderly relatives. Where was his Mrs? She scanned the crowd leaving the chapel and Mrs Fletcher wasn't part of it.

'Douglas's mother isn't here. Do you think she's fallen ill? Surely she hasn't been smitten by the angel too,' she whispered to Eileen and Lottie.

She followed the crowd looking for someone who might know the latest news of Mrs Fletcher. John Kelly was talking to Bert so she searched for Ginnie, she might know what had happened. Ginnie wasn't there either. Well that was strange. Ginnie Kelly had missed a grand service at the chapel and she'd tell her so.

After the burial, Helen had a few words with Mr Fletcher who then asked her back to the house but she made her excuses. Matt was walking her back to Granny Simpson's for tea and they were going to break the news of their Christmas plans. Her mam and dad were happy to have Matt stay with them. She hoped they'd like him as much as she did.

Ginnie sat with Dorothy, each lost in their own thoughts, until they heard voices approaching the front door. Dorothy sat up and retrieved a pill box from her pocket. Ginnie put her hand over the box. 'Dorothy, I don't think you need another. You may think they help but this is a day when people are remembering your son and you can't just sleepwalk through it all. Neville needs you there too.'

Dorothy put the box back in her pocket. 'Perhaps, you're right. They don't take the pain away, they just tuck it somewhere that's harder to reach. Let's go down and have tea.'

As soon as she could, Ginnie slipped away. The house was full of folk she didn't know and Ginnie seemed calmer. The poor woman. How would she get through Christmas without her bairn?

15

Once the twins were in bed, Ginnie started the final sleeve of Rose's cardigan. She was thankful that Rose was getting better. Recovery was slow and it would be a week or two before she was allowed home but she would come home, Ginnie was sure about that. She thought about Dorothy's fear of going to her son's burial and felt heartily sorry for the woman.

Her absence had caused some gossip that was for sure and Ginnie had almost fallen out with Edna over it when they were both collecting the boys from Mary's house. Edna Simpson had tried to pass judgement on the woman but she hadn't walked in her shoes, the shoes of fear and despair. It was easy for an outsider to say get over yourself.

One thing today had done was to make her determined to march through those hospital doors and see her girl from the inside corridor of the hospital this Saturday. The sixteenth was the last family visit before Christmas because the hospital hadn't enough staff on duty the weekend after. She'd buy an orange and bake some teacakes and take Rose another book from Miss Wakenshaw's pile. She couldn't wait to see Rose's bright smile.

John sat at the table cutting another sheet of thin white card into small rectangles. 'Have you plenty of card, pet?' she asked.

'Just enough for this list you've given me, lass. Mind you,

we seem to send a lot of Christmas greetings to folk we see every day.'

One of the good things about having an artist for a husband was that he made their Christmas cards. This year he was sketching in pencil and adding a touch of watercolour onto postcard size cards and they were writing their Christmas message on the back. Oil painting was his real love but it took time and space and, with Rose being so poorly and the weekend visits, he had hardly been at his shed on the allotment to paint over the past month.

She was proud of John being a 'pitman painter', part of the Ashington group who had shot to fame and even had exhibitions in London and in Edinburgh as well as Newcastle. A lot of their popularity was thanks to the patronage of Helen Sutherland who seemed to have money to burn and had treated many of the painters to a trip to London.

John hadn't gone on the trip because he didn't want to leave her with three little'uns and he was never in danger of letting a bit of local fame go to his head. 'Painting's easy,' he told her. 'Being part of the rescue team when there's a fall of stone and men are hurt, now that's tough and something I'm proud to do.'

The pitman painters were well known in the area and there were plenty of houses in these rows that proudly displayed one of John's paintings. He painted for love not for money but, occasionally, he sold a batch of paintings at the Armstrong Bridge Sunday market so he had money for more art supplies. His best paintings stayed with the Ashington group so their work could be shown together.

Ginnie didn't care for too much on the walls herself, a plain wallpaper with a clock and a mirror were sufficient for her, and some of his paintings were so dark and bleak. Who wanted miners sweating underground on their wall? Clearly, some folk did.

John was good at sketching the bairns playing, and he

caught their likeness too. She was fond enough of a sketch of Rose and the twins jumping a rope in their back yard to have it framed and sit on their dresser.

She did like the cheery sketches he was doing this month, fir trees, blazing fires and snowball fights adorned their Christmas cards.

'I don't know what to do for the Fletchers' card, Ginnie.' John sat with a pile of Christmas scenes just waiting for a touch of water colour.

Ginnie thought about it; it was a tricky one. 'Why not do a sketch of Douglas? Instead of writing a Merry Christmas message we could wish them peace, something like that.'

John came over and kissed her on the brow. 'Ginnie you're a genius. I'll need to get hold of a photo though. I wouldn't want it to be a bad likeness. I'll have a word with Mr Fletcher, test the water so to speak.'

Ginnie finished her line and put her knitting away as John tidied up his piles of card. It had been a hard day what with the funeral, Dorothy having a bit of a turn and then Edna shooting her mouth off, but it also brought home how lucky she was to have three lovely bairns and a man like John.

There was always one dark cloud. As she got undressed for bed, she thought of her mother and checked her breasts. She let out a breath of relief, no lumps yet and she was approaching the age her mother had been when she became ill.

Oh for a day without one worry or another. Maybe, God willing, her luck would stretch to seeing her bairns grow up after all.

16

Edna kept a sharp eye on Alfie and the girls. They didn't play out after school anymore and Alfie only mixed with the twins from number one. The angel was still hovering around the rows and nobody was safe.

Sixteen Linwood bairns were in the isolation hospital and there were more filling the wards from Burnside. Edna thanked the Lord every day for Eileen, Lottie and Alfie staying healthy, so far, and for Sid's arrival home today. His bed was all made up, his clothes were airing on the clothes horse in front of the fire and she would have those hospital clothes off him as soon as he set foot in the house.

When the ambulance pulled up she was sure the whole street could hear her heart thudding.

'Hello Mam, I'm back,' he grinned and she rushed to take him in her arms.

'You certainly are and you have no idea how pleased we are to have you here.'

She hugged him until he said, 'Mam! You're worse than the strangling angel. I can't breathe.'

She released him and took his hand to take him inside. 'I'm a bit old for hand holding, Mam.' He pulled away and marched in himself.

Edna had to satisfy herself with looking at him, giving his hair the odd stroke and making sure he was warm enough.

Her little lad had lost weight, *look at those spindly legs*. She would feed him up so he'd be back to his old self in no time.

She tried giving him a glass of milk. 'Ugh, Mam you know I don't like milk. I just like it with a biscuit or cake or I canna drink it.' He pushed her offering away.

In the afternoon, before the rest came in from their last day of school, he slept under a knitted blanket on the cushioned chair she'd drawn up to the fire. It had been a tiring day for him. Now was her chance to sit on the arm of the chair, trace the contours of his face and plant a kiss on his brow. 'I love you son,' she whispered and tears flowed down her cheeks when she thought of how this may have turned out.

She decided to make Sid's favourite biscuits. She hadn't made them for more than a year because they took up too much of the butter and sugar ration but her lad needed feeding up. She gathered together the ingredients, yes she'd have enough to make a batch and feed him a couple every day with a glass of milk.

As she creamed the butter and sugar, she thought of Mrs Fletcher. The funeral last week had brought home to Edna just how lucky she was and she'd have to go and say sorry to Ginnie for sounding off about Mrs Fletcher not being there.

Edna knew when she was in the wrong and, when she had time to think about what Ginnie had said to her, she felt a bit ashamed of judging Douglas's mother. It might be the proper thing to stand and mourn your son but not everyone was strong enough, and she didn't have to find out whether she was strong enough or not, thanks to her prayers being answered.

Edna enjoyed rolling the biscuit dough into small balls and flattening them with a fork dipped in cold water. After putting them in the oven, she set about preparing the evening meal. The biscuits would just take a few minutes so she kept an eye on them as she peeled taties.

The sweet smell told her when they were ready. She took

the biscuits out of the oven and placed them on a tray to cool. Those biscuits would tempt anybody to eat and her lad needed flesh on his bones.

Sid's eyes opened. 'Mam, what's that you're baking? It smells lovely and I sort of remember it.'

'I've baked you some buttery biscuits because you used to love them with a glass of milk. You'll have some every day to build you up.'

'Can I try them now?' Sid sat up and looked longingly at the tray.

'You certainly can, bonny lad.' Edna watched as he polished off two biscuits and drained the glass of milk.

She said another silent prayer of thanks because her son had been saved as she finished off preparing her family's evening meal. She'd pop around and make amends to Ginnie when it was in the oven.

17

Ginnie tucked the postcard sized sketch of Douglas in cricket whites with a bat under his arm into an envelope to keep it clean. John had caught the lad's stance and his grin and his happy nature. 'Dorothy will love this, John. I'll pop around with it tomorrow. I hope she's better; I haven't seen her since the day of the funeral.'

John glanced up from his sketch. 'You two are getting pally. I never thought I'd see the day when my wife was a regular caller at the big house.' He gave her a long look and his hand travelled over the paper in front of him in quick strokes. Ginnie could tell he was working on her likeness.

'It's strange. She's a lonely woman and I think she listens to me but I'm not going to make a habit of going there. I know my place and I don't mean that in a… in a… oh I don't know the word I'm looking for.'

'Subservient?'

'That'll do, it sounds right. I don't mean it in a subservient way but I'm not comfortable there. She needs somebody at the moment and nobody in her family seems to have stepped up, so I will.'

'It's your Christian duty,' John smiled.

'Don't you be mocking the chapel, John. You and your doubts and thinking.'

'I'd never mock you Ginnie,' he said. 'Look!' He showed

her a sketch of herself all gussied up in the way Mrs Fletcher dressed and she had to laugh. 'You'd fit in anywhere Ginnie, my love, because you have a kind heart and know who you are.'

'Edna Simpson showed a kinder side to herself today. She came and apologised for judging Dorothy the day of the funeral and said I'd been right to call her out on it.'

'She got Sid home today didn't she? She'll be counting her blessings. Oh for the day when our Rose is back.'

'She's on the mend and I'm so glad I saw that for myself last week.'

'You were brave to overcome that phobia of yours and I'm proud of you.' John gathered his cards and pencils together. 'Mr Fletcher lent me a good photograph of Douglas for the card. When I told him what I was doing, he asked if I could do a proper portrait of him from the likeness for Christmas. I said it would have to be pastels to be ready in time and I'd try my best.'

'Dorothy would love that. It is short notice, though. Are you sure you have time?' Ginnie asked.

'I thought I'd start it tomorrow and finish it early Sunday, but I've looked at the pastels I've got and it's a poor collection now. There's no way I can get that red hair and skin tone of the lad. I think it'll just have to be a pencil sketch.'

Ginnie stood up and went to the dresser. Should she? He'd have nothing for Christmas but he needed them now. 'John, here's your Christmas present. Open it early.'

John took the gift. 'Are you sure?'

Ginnie nodded.

He opened a new box of pastels with the assorted colours he needed.

After clearing away the breakfast dishes and waving John and the boys off to the allotment, Ginnie hung the iron girdle over the fire to heat. She quickly mixed a scone dough added a handful of currants and cooked a batch of singing hinnies on the girdle. Their singing told her just when to turn them over and, as soon as they were ready, she set off to the big house with the card and her batch of warm scones wrapped in a clean tea towel.

She knocked on the door and waited awhile until Mr Fletcher opened it up. 'Ah, Mrs Kelly, we weren't expecting visitors.' He looked grey and unshaven and unsure of what to do.

'I called to bring you a card and to see how Dorothy is keeping.' Was he going to keep her standing at the door? Maybe she shouldn't have knocked and just posted the card.

'I'm afraid Dorothy is still in bed. She isn't doing very well,' he said.

'May I visit her?'

'It's a bit of a mess and I'm not sure if she's up to visitors.' He hovered and Ginnie took action. 'If you don't mind, I'll pop up to see her and I'll do a few jobs if they're needed. That's what neighbours are for.'

He stepped aside, Ginnie left her basket on a chair in the hall and asked, 'Is she upstairs?

He nodded and added, 'If you're here with Dorothy, I'll go out for a short while.' Mr Fletcher grabbed his coat, clearly glad to get out of the house.

Dorothy was dressed and sitting on Douglas's bed looking into space. She had a brush and hand mirror in her hands but her hair wasn't in its usual neat victory roll. Ginnie took the brush, 'Here let's get this hair looking right.'

'I can't seem to leave this room. I can't bear the thought of Christmas or carrying on without him.'

Ginnie took a breath. She felt heartily sorry for Dorothy but carrying on like this would make her worse. 'What do you think Douglas would say if he saw his mother without her hair done at eleven in the morning? I don't suppose you've made up the fire or given his dad his breakfast either?'

Dorothy was silent for a while as Ginnie finished her hair. Had she gone too far?

'Do you think he's looking down on us? Do you believe that Ginnie?'

Ginnie put down the brush and held out the hand mirror for Dorothy to see the finished look. 'I don't rightly know and none of us can but just think of it as if he can. Show him you're alright because that's what he'd want. Look after his room but give these toys to bairns who will enjoy them.'

'I couldn't do that. They are all I have left.' Tears filled Dorothy's red and swollen eyes.

'No, you have memories. Ten years of wonderful memories so be glad of the years you had as well as sad for the years you have lost.'

'I believe you are telling me off,' Dorothy hung her head.

'No I wouldn't do that. I'm just trying to jog you along a bit. I'm worried for Mr Fletcher, he has an important job here and the men rely on him and I'm worried for you if you sit and mope too long. We pit women keep our tears for the long dark nights and just get on with things during the day because we have to be strong.'

'I don't make a very good pit woman, then.'

'It's a pretence at first. Pretend and the strength becomes real. I'm sure soldiers are the same.'

'You want me to give it a try?'

'I do. Anyway, when we've tidied up, I have a lovely sketch of Douglas to show you. John has drawn a good likeness. Let's get things put straight in the kitchen then we can enjoy a cup of tea and look at the card.

When Neville walked in an hour later, his face brightened at the fire blazing on the range, Dorothy up and dressed and Ginnie's plate of singing hinnies on the table.

'Come and have a cup of tea Neville, and look at the

drawing of Douglas in his cricket whites.' Dorothy was smiling and Ginnie was relieved to have helped. There would be other bad days of course but this was a start.

Ginnie took Neville to one side as Dorothy cleared the tea-cups and carried them into the scullery. She had a list of jobs for him. He had to take a long shopping list to the store with their ration books and ask for it all to be delivered by tea-time. After that, the shops would be closed until Wednesday. He then had to go into town and find a Christmas tree and something for Dorothy for Christmas day. Before coming home, he had to call at the Dodds' house to pay for a Christmas chicken. Ginnie was taking charge but he looked grateful to her.

'Dorothy, I'm staying with you until Mr Fletcher returns and I think we should pack up Douglas's Christmas presents and give them to some bairns who will be delighted with them. What do you say to that?' Ginnie wondered whether she might have moved a bit too quickly.

To her surprise, Dorothy nodded, saying, 'I can't get rid of his old toys in his room yet but I can do that with the new things I bought. I don't want unopened presents left in the house.'

18

Ginnie made sure Dorothy wrapped up warmly before they set off because the heavy sky signalled it might snow before the day was over. Third Row was their first stop.

When she knocked on the door of the Dodds' house, Mrs Dodd filled the doorway, with steam escaping from around her. 'Mr Fletcher will be calling later this afternoon to order and pay for that spare Christmas chicken you keep,' she informed Mrs Dodd. Mr Dodd always kept at least one aside so he could charge top whack for a last minute buy.

Mrs Dodd folded her arms, 'He'll be charged the Christmas Eve price. It's supply and demand you know.'

Ginnie nodded. 'Maybe Danny could deliver it over tomorrow morning with your other orders?'

'I'll see that he does,' Mrs Dodd looked over Ginnie's shoulder towards Dorothy who seemed to be hiding behind her thick scarf, 'I'm sorry for your loss Mrs Fletcher. It's terrible to lose a bairn.'

Dorothy stepped forward and handed Mrs Dodd a package wrapped in tartan paper. 'Thank you. Would you accept this extra gift for Danny? I have no need for it now.'

Mrs Dodd seemed lost for words for a moment. 'Thank you, an extra present won't go amiss.'

As they left, Ginnie explained, 'That magpie's scarf has gone to a good home. Young Danny loves his football and he'll be thrilled to have something new. He's the youngest of four lads so he always wears his brothers' hand-me-downs.'

Their next call was the Irwins. The two oldest lads were in the isolation hospital until after Christmas but there were three girls and a little lad who wouldn't be getting much because Mr Irwin was too fond of a bet on the horses.

'We'd better not go inside today even if we're asked because the Irwins are usually lifting,' Ginnie explained.

'Lifting what?' Dorothy frowned.

Ginnie laughed. 'Lifting. Lifting with lice.'

Dorothy's eyes widened and then she laughed too. 'Whatever would Neville say if I went home lifting.'

They were both still laughing when the door opened and a small girl peered from behind it. 'Mam says she's out.'

Ginnie crouched to the level of the suspicious eyes. 'She says that does she? Will you go back and tell her to come to the door because Father Christmas has sent her a message,'

Little feet flew across the floorboards and called up the stairs, 'Mam, come down it's a wife with a message from Father Christmas.'

Mrs Irwin came to the door looking pale and tired. Ginnie could see she was expecting again. 'Jean, I was wondering if you could make use of a few wrapped presents for the bairns? Mrs Fletcher, you know she lost her lad last week, can't stand the sight of them under her tree and wants to find them a good home.'

'Here please take them, take the basket too, I don't need it, it's an old one.' Mrs Fletcher held out the basket of presents..

Jean took it. 'I've been saying my rosary hoping that Pete would come home before the shops shut for Christmas, bring home some winnings for a change. I've got the Christmas dinner put by but nothing wrapped for the bairns. I was going to buy them some sweets for their stockings if he got back before closing.' She peered into the basket. 'All these?'

Mrs Fletcher smiled. 'Yes. There's a *Dandy* annual, a circus jigsaw, a toy tank, a colouring book and wax crayons.'

'I'll hide them away until Christmas morning. This'll be one they won't forget.' Some life came back into Jean's pale face. 'Thanks, Mrs Fletcher and I'm so sorry about Douglas. I know my older boys were down by the burn with Dougie and it's a crying shame you've only the one and he's gone.'

Mrs Fletcher gave a brisk nod and walked off.

'Have I said something wrong, Ginnie?' Jean asked.

'I think you said the right thing but she gets upset just at the mention of Douglas. Enjoy your Christmas, Jean.' Ginnie followed Dorothy who was dabbing at her eyes.

'Those poor children. I lost one baby after another and could have provided for them all and there is that desperate woman, carrying again, who can hardly feed and clothe the brood she's got.'

'That's because her man, Peter Irwin, wastes his hard earned pay packet on the horses and keeps on getting her pregnant. She was a bonny lass and very much in love when they got married. A good man is a blessing and we both have one of those Dorothy.' She linked Dorothy's arm. 'One more call with this.' Ginnie held up her shopping bag with the wrapped Meccano set peeping from the top.

'Don't you want it for the twins?'

'They'd love it but I think Sidney Simpson deserves a present for being the first bairn home from hospital to his family. Do you mind?'

'I think that's a wonderful idea but will you take it around later? I'd like to get back home now.'

Ginnie could see that Dorothy was sapped of energy. She stayed until Neville returned and then set off to the Simpsons'.

'I have something but I don't want Sid to see it,' she whispered when Edna came to the door.

'Come in. Sid is upstairs reading with Alfie. They're enjoying having the fire lit in the bedroom. I'm keeping him warm, there's not a picking of fat on him so he'll feel the cold.'

Ginnie stepped in and handed the box, wrapped in tartan and a blue ribbon, to Edna.

'What's this?' Edna asked.

'Mrs Fletcher is giving Douglas's presents away. She doesn't want them there at Christmas.'

Edna frowned and crossed her arms. 'I'm not in need of charity, Ginnie Kelly. I have our own presents put away for all the bairns.'

Ginnie rolled her eyes. Why couldn't Edna just accept a gift? 'I didn't say you were in need of anything, Mrs Fletcher is the one in need. She's is in need of some help to get through Christmas. Seeing as Sidney is the first bairn to come home from the hospital, first bairn alive anyway, she wants him to have the Meccano set.'

'A Meccano set?' He didn't even ask for that because they're pricey but I know he wanted one.' She took the large box. 'Are you sure? What about your twins?'

'They haven't been poorly and Sid has. Just accept it and be happy Edna, for heaven's sake.' Ginnie was hungry and it had been a tiring afternoon.

'I will then. Shall I say it would've been Douglas's?'

'Don't be soft. Tell him it was from Father Christmas.'

Ginnie was exhausted with it all and glad to get home. The twins had been fed, bathed and were in their nightclothes and John was boiling fresh water on the range. 'I thought, after you've had some of that lovely pie you made, you might like a quiet bath while I put the twins to bed and tell them a story.'

She ate a slice of pie, drank a cup of strong black tea and thought about Jean Irwin waiting for her husband to arrive home and praying his pockets weren't empty. John was a good man and look what he'd done while she was out. She studied the portrait of Douglas he was working on. It wasn't complete but, already, she could see his features emerging and John had blended the colours to the exact russet of his curly hair. John was making something that the Fletchers would treasure.

19

Dorothy chatted about her day to Neville as they hung decorations on the Christmas tree he'd brought home.

He stepped back to look at the tree. 'It's a bit straggly, I think all the best ones had been taken but it'll look fine when we've added the rest of the baubles and lights, don't you think?'

'I do, Neville.' Dorothy sat back on her knees to admire their work so far. 'This morning, I couldn't have contemplated a tree but now I've given away Douglas's gifts and seen how some of those little ones live, I feel like I have no right spread my misery around everyone else.

We gave Douglas ten happy Christmases and he gave us so much. I want to remember the happy times we had instead of dwelling on what we will miss.' Dorothy hoped her heart was listening to her head's sensible words because inside she still felt empty and aching.

Reality hit her the moment she opened her eyes, Christmas Eve and no Douglas. Dorothy dragged herself out of bed to light the fire and make a pot of tea. The tree glistened with tinsel in the corner so she turned on its lights and felt cheered. The loss of Douglas was devastating but she had to make it bearable and she had to get through Christmas for Neville's sake.

A loud knock at the door jolted her from thoughts of last Christmas eve and she opened it to find a cheery faced lad holding a large bird. 'You look like someone out of a Charles Dickens novel,' she laughed.

'Who's he when he's at home?' the lad asked as he tried to hand her the chicken.

Dorothy stepped aside. It wasn't wrapped but at least it was plucked. 'Could you carry it through and put it on the bench?' she asked.

'I could but will you watch my wheelbarrow? There's five more in there and I don't want them to disappear. You have to watch some folk, you know.'

Dorothy pulled her robe around her and watched the barrow wondering just how she would stop anyone who came along and helped themselves. The lad came back and thanked her. 'Wait there,' she dashed back into the kitchen and took a silver sixpence from her purse. His face lit up with delight when she handed it to him.

'My name's Danny, Danny Dodd and if you need any jobs doing now you've lost your Dougie just give me a shout. I won't expect a tanner every time either. You're a canny woman Mrs Fletcher, Merry Christmas.' He picked up the handles of his barrow and he was off.

Well. Dorothy wasn't sure whether to laugh or cry, now she had lost her Dougie indeed. She closed the door, rested her back against it and thought over what he had said. She had to smile, that Danny Dodd was a character and she was glad he would be the one to wear Douglas's scarf on Christmas Day.

Neville came downstairs, 'Who was that on a Sunday morning?'

'It's not any Sunday, it's Christmas Eve and we've had tomorrow's chicken delivered. There's a pot of tea brewing and the fire is blazing so let's have some breakfast.'

After breakfast, Dorothy opened the back door to fill the coal scuttle and saw it lying there by the back gate. A wreath of holly with red berries, pine cones and Christmas roses in their yard. 'Neville! Neville what's this doing in the yard?'

Neville stood in the doorway looking ashen. 'Sorry Dorothy it's me. I bought it yesterday but didn't want to bring it in and upset you. I'm taking it to the cemetery this afternoon.'

She turned back into the house and climbed upstairs. She felt safe in Douglas's room. One step forward and she was crashing back. She reached into her apron pocket for her pills. No! Not that route, she wouldn't go back into that half-world. She flung the pills aside and gave in to a good weep.

A little while later, feeling better for the tears, she went downstairs. 'Neville love, it's a caring thought so please go and place the wreath on Douglas's… in Douglas's spot. I can't go with you yet but I will one day. I'm just not ready. I feel him in his room and would rather remember him there.'

'I understand sweetheart, I really do. I'll take it myself.'

Would life always be this hard for them? Memories of Douglas, no other children? Dorothy would just try to get through today.

Dorothy must have fallen asleep on Douglas's bed because it was dusk when she heard singing. 'Hark! The Herald Angels Sing' drifted up from the street. She sat up to look out of the window and there in the half-light with lanterns aglow stood the chapel carol singers. Eddie the accordion player, the deacon and Miss Wakenshaw lead a group of adults and children in the singing.

Walking downstairs, she found Neville standing at the open door and singing along with them. She found her voice and joined in. These were the angels to sing about and rejoice in. The strangling angel of diphtheria had taken her boy and she only hoped he was with these angels and could hear her singing out right now.

As they were standing at the door listening to a cheery 'Ding Dong Merrily on High', John Kelly came up to the house and handed Neville a wrapped parcel. 'All done, Mr Fletcher.'

Neville took it saying, 'Come into the house and tell me what I owe you.'

'It was a labour of love. I can't possibly take a penny.'

'You must, John. I wouldn't have taken your time otherwise.'

John shook his head. 'Put it into the chapel collection box, Mr Fletcher. Merry Christmas.' He disappeared into the darkening street.

John walked out into the dusk in search of the collection box just as the group started moving away. This was the last house in Linwood and the carollers would have to put out their lanterns and head home soon because of the blackout rules. What had John Kelly brought Neville?

20

Jean Irwin got up early to light the range before the bairns got up. A Sunday morning, Christmas Eve, and she was looking forward to the day. The morning sickness had stopped at last so she had more energy, and yesterday's act of kindness by Mrs Fletcher had perked her up no end.

Yesterday, when the two women left, Jean had boiled pans for bath water and the four little'uns had endured a scrub in the tub by the fire. She'd shaved her little lad's head and had used the evil smelling lotion that Mary Elliot had made up for her in the summer to treat the girls' hair. Oh how the lassies had tutted and fussed as she used the fine tooth comb to pull out fleas and nit eggs but, once they'd all had their hair rinsed in vinegar and warm water and rolled into rags, they were happy enough.

'We'll have ringlets for Christmas won't we, Mam?' her eldest tossed the rags that were curling her hair over her shoulder.

'Yes, you will and Father Christmas might bring you something else.' Jean smiled at the thought of them waking up on Monday morning to the gifts she'd taken from Mrs Fletcher.

Today was a Sunday, some folk in the rows would frown but she was going to clean the house and send Pete to find a fir tree from somewhere. What was the use of presents if there was no tree to put them under?

Pete wasn't getting any money, she only had a copper or two in her purse until next pay day, so he'd have to dig one up. It was no good giving him money anyway because, even on a Sunday, he'd find something to bet on. She loved her man but he couldn't be relied on if he had anything jingling in his pocket. She went to the stairs and called him, 'Pete time to get up. We have jobs to do and no time to waste.'

By teatime, Jean looked around her shabby kitchen with her chin held high. The mats were threadbare and the curtains were thin but the nets at the windows were white, the floor was clean and her range was sparkling. Her four bairns were tucking into a bowl of soup with a national loaf to fill them.

The girls had their shiny ringlets tied back with some ribbons she'd unearthed while cleaning and little Harry had a nicely shaped head so his shaved look wasn't so bad. Her bairns were as bonny as any in the rows.

In her larder was their Christmas dinner. She could only dream of a chicken but she'd scraped together enough for the butcher to put something by for her. Hadn't he kept her some of his best sausages? She was making roast potatoes with vegetables and a toad in the hole. A big Yorkshire pudding with eight sizzling sausages would be their Christmas treat after they'd opened their presents.

Jean sat back into the armchair exhausted but, as she sipped a cup of tea, her heart was almost bursting what with the excitement of tomorrow and her love for her brood. If only the two bigger lads were here. They'd be well cared for at the isolation hospital but it would have been lovely to have them home for all their fighting and cussing.

At least she had a houseful of little'uns and hadn't lost a bairn, yet. Her heart broke for Mrs Fletcher. She wouldn't swap Mrs Fletcher's place in that fine house of hers for all the tea in the Co-op.

The back door opened bringing a gust of cold air and she turned to see a huge tree staggering into the scullery with Pete behind it. He put it down panting. 'Isn't this a corker, hinnie?'

'Don't bring that in here until you've cleaned its roots and put it in a tub, Peter Irwin!' Jean jumped up in dismay. Her clean lino!

Pete backed out with the tree and she could hear him grumbling, 'I find the finest tree around, cut it down and carry it home to be shouted at. What's a man to do?'

The bairns rushed out to look at the tree and Jean followed. She hugged Peter. 'It's a grand tree. Sometimes you do something right, pet and I love you for it.'

Jean hugged her arms around herself as she watched Pete and the bairns go off to the allotment to find a tub for the tree. They would have a night of decorating the tree and listening to the radio while she sat by her sparkling range. She could hardly wait for the bairns to go up to bed and then she could put out those presents. 1944 was going to be a Christmas the Irwins would remember.

21

On Christmas Eve, Helen and Matt were sitting on the back seat of a packed bus going to Rothbury. Their overnight bags were stuffed into the overhead luggage rack and a bagful of presents sat squashed between them. 'I've wrapped chocolates for your mother and a half bottle of whiskey for your father. Will that be all right?' Matt asked.

'You didn't need to, I've already got them presents but it is really kind and they'll be delighted. Have you used up all of your coupons?'

'No, I had enough for these too.' Matt produced a quarter of chocolate eclairs for the journey.

They sat in comfortable silence looking out of the window while chewing their sweets, when Matt said, 'Tell me why some folk get over a bout of diphtheria and some don't.'

Helen drew in a deep breath. 'Where do I start?' she said more to herself than to Matt. She turned towards him and sat forward. 'It's highly infectious and can close the throat so some patients can choke to death. It depends on the size of the solid grey deposits, they form something called the pseudo-membrane.'

'Can't you remove it?' Matt asked.

'The grey coating is there because the bacteria has destroyed the top layers of the throat's mucosa and any attempt to remove it causes serious bleeding. An added complication is the neck swelling leading to airway obstruction that way too. I suppose that's why it's been named the strangling angel of children.'

'Some do recover, what is different for the rest?'

'We can give an antitoxin and some respond better than others. We can help to clear the airway by putting a hole in the windpipe and inserting a tube, a tracheostomy, in the throat but with many patients the toxin travels away from the throat to the heart or liver or another organ. This leads to more complications that result in death. Infecting others and the chance of complications is why we keep the children in hospital for so long.'

'It seems a nasty, complicated illness, I'm pleased you've had the vaccine.' Matt said.

'It is nasty yet there is a solution to all this. It is taking time to roll out to all areas and it's frustrating it has taken so long.'

'What can be done, Helen?' Matt held her gaze, waiting for her opinion.

Helen sighed. So much could be done but progress was slow. 'We've made a start because the Beveridge Report made recommendations about disease and this year's white paper has set out principles for setting up a national health service. Once this war is over, we can get a health service up and running and we will be able to ensure the diphtheria vaccine gets to everywhere it should go.' Her cheeks felt flushed when she finished. A better health service was something she was passionate about.

'I didn't know much of that. Thanks Helen. The sooner we see an end to this war and improve lives in this country, the better.'

Matt cared about the things she cared about and he listened. As he clasped her hand and gave it a gentle squeeze, Helen realised she was falling in love.

They'd eaten supper with Mam and Dad and chatted by the fire about local news. 'They've rebuilt the Jubilee Hall, at last. Made a good job of it too but it hasn't got the reading room anymore.' Dad told them as he smoked his pipe.

Helen explained to Matt, 'The hall was used a lot but burnt down a few years ago after a Saturday film show and it's a big miss around here.'

'Humphrey Bogart was in it but I forget which film,' Mam added.

'1939 it was, the fire,' Dad informed them. 'They got their finger out at last and re-built it because the army need it as a centre for troops. We'll get it back once this war is all over.'

The clock struck ten and as regular as the clock, Dad said, 'Well, it's time for me to go up to my bed. Lovely meeting you Matt and I hope you sleep well above the forge.'

'I'll take Matt over and show him where he's sleeping,' Helen said.

'You'll need a torch because it's pitch black out there. It's almost a full moon but it's covered by snow clouds. I dare say there will be snow tonight.' Dad opened the cupboard for a torch.

'Get two out pet,' Mam suggested. 'Matt will need one over there and Helen will need one to see herself back to the door.'

They took the torches and, as they left, Mam said, 'I'll sit up and wait to see you're safely back across the yard.'

That would be her chance to ask Mam what she thought. She hoped she liked Matt. Both of her parents seemed to.

After showing Matt his bed she said goodnight and, as she was about to leave, he put his hand on her shoulder. 'Wait a moment, Helen.'

She shivered, it was chilly above the forge when the fire wasn't blazing below. Matt pulled her closer into his arms saying, 'You're cold.'

He radiated heat. He mustn't feel the cold. She enjoyed the warmth, the closeness and wasn't in any hurry to move out of his embrace.

'I've really enjoyed tonight. Your parents, they're lovely folk and thank you for the invitation.'

'I'm happy you came. It seems to me like we've known each other for more than a few weeks. Do you feel the same?' Her heart thudded waiting for his response. This couldn't be one-sided could it?

'I feel like I've met someone very special and I wanted to give you this while we were alone.' He handed her a small box.

She opened it with fumbling fingers as he held the torch. A heart-shaped locket. Silver on a silver chain. It was beautiful and she impulsively reached up to kiss his cheek. He turned and their lips met.

He kissed her softly briefly and pulled away. Their eyes locked and their lips met again, a delicious, slow, warm and breathtaking kiss. Helen's tummy cartwheeled with pleasure and she gasped as they parted.

'Merry Christmas, Helen.' He released her and took a step back.

'Merry Christmas.' Helen's blush was hidden by the dim light of the torch. 'I'd better go. Mam will be wondering if I've got lost.'

He chuckled, 'I think your mother will know exactly what we're doing. She was young once. Sleep well, Helen. I love you.'

He loved her! Her feet flew over the yard and she turned off the torch as she entered the kitchen.

'By your cheeks look rosy, our Helen. Is it chilly out there?' Mam asked. 'Come and sit down by the fire and let's catch up on how your nursing is going.'

22

On Christmas morning Maisie and Betty Johnson called at First Row to take the twins to the children's carol service at the chapel and Ginnie waved them off thinking it was strange not to see Rose walking along with them. Oh, she'd miss her today.

The Irwin bairns passed by with their dad. Under their wool hats, the three lassies all had their hair in ringlets. He must be taking them along to the chapel while Jean made the dinner. 'Merry Christmas, Ginnie,' he called.

'Merry Christmas, Pete.' He wasn't a bad sort, if only the bookies weren't his weakness.

She was about to go back inside when Danny Dodd skidded to a halt in front of her on an old bike that was slightly too big for him. 'Look at what I got for Christmas, Mrs Kelly! It's fourth hand but it goes well and I'm going to try it out properly on a long ride this afternoon.'

'It's a real bobby dazzler, Danny,' Ginnie said as he hopped off and propped it by her door. 'The sky looks heavy, there might be snow later, mind you.'

'I don't mind a bit of snow. Did you remember I was calling for Christmas messages for Rose? I'm testing my bike out by riding all the way to the hospital and back after I've had my dinner.' Danny wore the new magpies football scarf from Dorothy Fletcher around his neck and the biggest grin. 'It means

I'll miss my dad snoring after dinner and having to listen to the King's Christmas message with my mam and Gracie.'

Ginnie went into the kitchen and picked up a message she had written, a note from Mary, the cards the twins had drawn and John's sketch. He had drawn their kitchen range and Christmas tree with Rose and the twins sitting on the mat by the fire. Rose would love seeing that. 'Here you are Danny. It's very kind of you but I'm not sure if you'll get to the hospital door today.'

'I'll not just get there, I'll knock and say there's a special delivery for Rose Kelly. I'll bang until they take notice. Merry Christmas, Mrs Kelly,' he said and he was off.

Shortly after that, John walked over to the 'tute to meet his marras. All the men from the rows would be at the bar of the working men's institute for an hour this morning because the winding wheel of the pit was having a day of rest. No rest for the women, though. It was time she and Mary-from-next-door started on the dinner.

When Christmas came, Ginnie and Mary were a team. This year, they were cooking for six adults and four bairns so they'd pooled their allotment vegetables for a good selection, shared one of the chickens that Mr Dodd kept on his allotment and were making a giant Christmas plum duff with custard. From ten in the morning, they prepared and cooked the dinner using their two ranges to get everything ready at the same time. At one, they would serve up together, but they always ate in their own houses because there were too many of them to sit around one table.

Mr Elliot hadn't gone to the 'tute with John this year because he'd been poorly. He had the black lung from years down the pit and he'd told them all that he was happy to sit at his own hearth, sip a bottle of beer and wait for his grandbairns to arrive. The Elliots' son, Larry, and his wife and two bairns would walk from Burnside and be ready for their lunch at one o' clock.

Dorothy listened to the radio, prepared dinner for Neville and herself and kept taking a long look at the pastel portrait of Douglas. It had been a wonderful surprise this morning! John Kelly had caught her son's expression and it eased her heart looking at it. She was going through the motions of living and trying not to think of the long days that stretched ahead without that boy who had brought her such joy, but the kindness of people like the Kellys helped.

This morning's news told of how doodlebugs meant for Manchester had resulted in forty-four deaths and over a hundred injuries in the surrounding area. In one street of Oldham, twenty-seven were killed. How would the rest of the folk in Abbey Hills Road feel today? War and disease meant there were many more mothers like herself who were facing up to being childless and many of them would be homeless too so she mustn't let herself slide into another well of despair.

She took the chicken out of the oven. Look at the size of it! Far too much for her and Neville even if they ate it for a few days. On impulse, she cut off a leg and a few slices of one breast and put it between two plates then wrapped the plates in a tea towel. After scrawling a quick note, 'There is far too much for us. Please take this to save it going to waste. DF', she slipped along to leave it on the Irwins' front step. She had to get through Christmas as best she could but at least she could make those children's day better.

Helen helped her mother to cook dinner whilst Dad took Matt to The Queen's Arms. 'Your dad has taken a shine to your young man. Are you two serious?' Mam asked.

'I'm falling for him, Mam. He's so lovely to be with and we both seem to feel the same. Last night he told me he loved me but I haven't said it back, yet. I think I do.'

'What about your nursing? If you're serious and he proposes, you can't still nurse. It's what you've always wanted.'

Her mam dried her hands on her apron and poured a glass of sherry for them both.

'I haven't given that much thought. I know the rules and they seem unfair for this day and age. Why married women can't nurse, I don't know.'

'Rules are rules and it will be a hard choice so you'd better give it some thought, pet.'

'Maybe, once the war is over, the rules will change. Wouldn't that be marvellous?'

'It would, but don't bank on it Helen.'

Helen loved nursing and she loved Matt so she couldn't imagine giving either of them up but today wasn't the day to worry about that. She touched the locket at her neck. Today was a day to enjoy together.

Edna took Eileen and Lottie to the early church service and Bert watched over Sid and Alfie. Edna didn't want Sid to go outdoors yet. Their congregation prayed for the poor Lancashire folk who had been plagued by the doodlebugs for two nights in a row and had lost loved ones and their homes. They prayed that God would clip the wings of the strangling angel who had visited almost every family sitting in church today. Edna sometimes wondered how God could let such things happen but she quickly pushed her doubts aside. If her faith wore thin, she just had to look at her Sid who had been saved. She was thankful for that.

Jean was cooking the dinner while Pete went to the 'tute for an hour then collected the bairns from chapel. Jean had been soft and given him what was in her purse, just enough for a pint. It meant she could move from scullery to kitchen without any of them under her feet.

They'd had such a lovely morning. The bairns' cries of wonder at a few toys, their excitement at going to the chapel and telling the other bairns what they'd found from Father Christmas and the huge tree in the corner of the room made it the best Christmas that Jean could remember since being married.

Maybe this year, Peter would see how he was never going to get a big win and his bairns needed the money more than the bookies. She hoped so.

She went to the front door to see if they were coming along the street and found Dorothy's note and the roast chicken. She couldn't believe her good fortune. She'd serve this with half the sausages and they'd have bubble and squeak on boxing day with the rest. What a wonderful time this had turned out to be.

When one o' clock struck, Ginnie and Mary reached for their clean serving up pinnies. Their meal was ready. The air was rich with delicious smells and Mary took her share to be dished up next door.

The Kellys gathered around the table. 'Eat slowly and enjoy it. It takes hours to prepare and I don't want you gobbling it in minutes,' Ginnie said as she placed delicious plates of dinner in front of them.

'I wonder what Rose's dinner is like in hospital.' David speared one of his favourite roast potatoes adding, 'It won't be as good as yours, Mam.'

'Poor Rose, fancy missing this,' mumbled Stanley with a mouthful of chicken.

'Don't talk with your mouth full, son.' John caught Ginnie's eye and he gave her a wink. 'Sit down, lass. Enjoy this magnificent feast while it's hot.'

They hardly had room for the pudding, but they all took a spoonful and hoped to find a silver sixpence in there.

'Aha! Look what I've got.' John held up a shiny sixpence.

'How are you so lucky, Dad?' David asked.

'You find it every year. How do you do it?' Stanley's perplexed frown made Ginnie smile. John's sleight of hand with a tanner impressed all of the bairns. He was a regular Will Goldston when it came to finding a sixpence in the Christmas pudding or a penny in a birthday scone.

After dinner was cleared away, the Elliots, their son Larry and his family came around to the Kellys carrying their dining chairs to sit on. The room was packed to the gills so they could listen to the King on the wireless together and then play games.

It was almost three o'clock when Edna and Bert Simpson settled down in front of the fire and waited for the King's Christmas message, happy to be at home with all of their four bairns. Dorothy and Neville tuned in at the big house. Jean and Peter sat by their wireless with the bairns playing happily around their feet. Helen and Matt listened with the rest of the Tweedie clan in Rothbury. Danny Dodd slipped away from the adults in Third Row and cycled off to deliver Rose some Christmas messages of her own.

Christmas was celebrated in the rows in spite of doodlebugs and disease and each household experienced the joy of Christmas in small moments during the day. There was a feeling of hope in the air after listening to King George. Hadn't he said that the lamps which the Germans had put out all over Europe were being rekindled and beginning to shine? Perhaps this would be the last Christmas they were at war with the unwelcome angel and Mr Hitler. 1945 was just around the corner, perhaps it would be the year they conquered both.

If you enjoyed this novella, you may want to
read more about the Kelly family in a heart-wrenching
saga of love, family and secrets. *Rose's Choice* is the
first book in The Colliery Rows series.

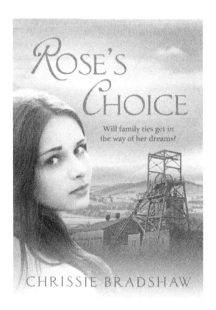

Rationing, bombing, disease and pit disasters are part of Rose
Kelly's World War Two childhood. When the spirited coalminer's daughter discovers a family secret, she makes a choice
that overshadows her teenage years. Rose tries to make the
most of post-war opportunities but a family tragedy pulls her
back to a life in the colliery rows. She relinquishes her bright
future for domestic duties because her family comes first.
Will family ties get in the way of her dreams?

LINWOOD LANGUAGE – A GLOSSARY

Adam's ale – a glass of water

Bait – a packed meal for taking to work

Bevin boy – a conscripted miner, named after Ernest Bevin

Clout – a smack or thump

Cloot – a rag or cloth

Clootie fruit pudding – a pudding filled with fruit and boiled in a cloth then left to dry by the fire before serving

Connie – conscientious objector, shortened from conscientious

Cracket – a low stool with a hole in the middle for carrying it around

Doylem – a foolish person

Gallowa – any pit pony not just a Galloway pony

Hinny – a term of endearment like 'honey'

Linties – fast running birds, so used to describe anyone rushing about

Lowse – finishing time, the end of a miner's shift or drinking up time at a bar

Lifting – crawling with lice

Marra – a workmate or friend

Masting – the brewing of tea in a pot

Netty – lavatory. Some say it is a shortening of 'necessary'

Nowt – nothing

Owt – anything

Plum duff – a spiced, steamed or boiled pudding

Pig's ear – a mess, 'you've made a pig's ear of that'

Proggy mat – a homemade mat made from pushing strips of cloth into a hessian backing with a progger

Progger – a tool for making a proggy mat

Scullery – a room off the kitchen with a sink, bench, some shelving and sometimes a larder

Singing hinny – a scone cooked on a girdle

Taties – potatoes

Tats – knots or tangles in hair or wool

Yammer – to moan and groan

RECIPES

Want to try some of the wartime cooking from the rows? Here are two recipes:

Sid's Buttery Biscuits

Ingredients:

- 150g flour – self raising, or add 2 teaspoons of baking powder to plain

- 100g butter

- 50g sugar

Method:

- Cream the sugar and butter together in a large bowl until pale and fluffy

- Add the flour a spoonful at a time and mix well

- Gather the mixture together with your hands to form a large ball

- Roll 14 small balls of soft dough with your hands (walnut sized)

- Place on a greased baking tray

- Gently press down on each ball with a fork dipped in cold water. This makes the biscuit shape and adds a pattern

- Cook in a hot (180 degrees) oven until golden (12 -15 minutes)

- Cool on a baking tray and store in an airtight container

Plum duff – a steamed winter pudding served with custard

Ingredients:

- Carrot and potato from the allotment adds bulk and, as this pudding is low in fat and sugar, it doesn't use a lot of rationed food.

- 75g grated carrot

- 100g grated potato

- 85g plain flour

- 1/2 cup or 30g breadcrumbs

- 30g shredded suet

- I teaspoon of spice – allspice, mixed spice or cinnamon

- 1 teaspoon of bicarbonate of soda

- 1 tablespoon of dried fruit (mixed, currants or raisins. Soak in hot water or, if it's Christmas, a drop of any spirit, for an hour)

- 2 tablespoons of warm water

Method:

- Take a large mixing bowl, add the carrot, potato, suet, flour, breadcrumbs and spice, and mix together.

- Dissolve the bicarbonate of soda in the warm water and add to the mixture

- Knead into a ball on a lightly floured surface. It may seem dry but it will come together after a few minutes of kneading

- Drain the mixed fruit and add to the mixture, making sure to work it evenly through the dough

- Make the dough into a ball or make two balls if you are making two smaller puddings

- Grease the pudding basin(s) and push the ball down so it fits half the bowl

- Cover the bowl with a clean cloot (rag) and tie it in place with string. If you have some, greased greaseproof paper may be used to cover the pudding before tying with the rag

- Make a handle for bowl by threading a double length of string through the string already tied around the pudding. Pull it through to the other side and secure. The pudding is now ready to go into the pan

- Place a saucer at the bottom of your pan for the basin to sit on

- Pour boiling water around to the rim of the basin but not over the top

- Cover with a lid and simmer the pudding in the water for 2 hours. Keep topping up the water

- When the pudding is steamed, lift it from the pan, cut the string from around the bowl and gently ease away the cloot and paper

Serve with hot custard or a white brandy sauce at Christmas

THE PITMEN PAINTERS
1934-84

The pitmen painters were a group of artists who formed in the 1930s. In 'The Unwelcome Angel', John Kelly is a fictional character from the group. The group began as an evening class of Northumbrian pitmen keen to learn about art. Within weeks they were producing their own work and, over the years, their paintings amounted to a complete record of life in a mining community: work at the coal face, the pithead baths, allotments, the pit ponies and scenes from the colliery rows. They were exhibited in London and Edinburgh as well as locally. William Feaver's book 'Pitmen Painters: The Ashington Group, 1934-1984' covers the fifty year history of the group and contains illustrations of dozens of paintings, drawings, prints and sculptures by the pitmen. Lee Hall of 'Billy Elliot' fame has written a successful play, 'The Pitmen Painters'. It has toured nationally and internationally. A large collection of the group's work is on display at Woodhorn Museum in Northumberland. As well as holding a fascinating exhibition of the pitmens' paintings, this old colliery site is packed full of the social history of mining and well worth a visit.

BOOKS IN THIS SERIES

THE COLLIERY ROWS

A series of family sagas set in Linwood Colliery rows

The Unwelcome Angel

A gripping emotional novella for readers who would love to read more about how the women coped in the winter of 1944 when the strangling angel visited Linwood. You'll learn more about the epidemic from Ginnie Kelly, Edna Simpson, Dorothy Fletcher and a new character, Nurse Helen Tweedie as they battle diphtheria, pit dust, the Germans and prepare for a World War 2 Christmas.

Rose's Choice

Rationing, bombing, disease and pit disasters are part of Rose Kelly's World War 2 childhood. When the spirited coalminer's daughter discovers a family secret, she makes a choice that overshadows her teenage years. Rose tries to make the most of post-war opportunities but family tragedy pulls her back to a life in the colliery rows. She relinquishes her bright future for domestic duties because her family comes first. Will family ties get in the way of her dreams?

Rose's Ever After

Coming out soon. A return to the colliery rows to meet Rose and the Kelly family again, including Joy. There are tears and triumphs in this moving saga of love and belonging.

OTHER BOOKS BY CHRISSIE BRADSHAW

A Jarful of Moondreams - Cleo has always strived for success and enjoys her independent lifestyle but she is about to lose control of her life and discover how tough that can be. Alex hates the crazy idea that she should be uprooted from her home and friends to live with Cleo, her bossy older sister. Teri is desperate for her two daughters to bond but worries that she has left it too late. Love and change is in the air and the 'Moondream' jar that has held their wishes for many years is about to spill shocking secrets. Follow Cleo, Teri and Alex as they face a summer to remember and discover just what it takes to make their dreams come true.

The Barn of Buried Dreams - Erin and Heather Douglas are struggling. Their mother's death has left a void in their family and everyday life has side-lined their dreams. Erin has buried herself away in the family home and left her stage career. By hiding away, she is avoiding the pain of returning to London and the acting world where her ex-fiancé is enjoying success and a new relationship. When she meets charismatic Texan Jackson McGee, she wrestles with her feelings for him. Should she trust another man? Heather is juggling babies, work, a rocky marriage and running on wine. An overheard conversation makes her ask, would Mark cheat on her? Can the sisters help one another to face their fears, dust off and revive those dreams and find joy in life?

PRAISE FOR AUTHOR

" A really enjoyable story that flows naturally. Lovely characters and descriptions. Highly recommend." AnneMarie Brear -saga writer

" Very well written and so true to life…"CB Staffs

"…lovely storyline and likeable characters. It will make you laugh and cry in equal measure. This is a very accomplished debut novel. I am really looking forward to her next book." - Book literati

"I knew, as soon as I started talking to the characters, I was hooked." Poppy

"Chrissie has a lovely writing style that is full of warmth and charm. Her description was seamless and instantly drew me in. The storyline flowed perfectly, it was tender and engaging which made for a compelling and addictive read.' Dash fan

"I was captivated from the start and wanted to keep on reading and reading. The author knows how to fill this book to the brim with emotions…in my opinion this was a very fluently written work of art." Els Ebraert B for Book Review

ABOUT THE AUTHOR
CHRISSIE BRADSHAW

Chrissie, 2016 winner of the Romantic Novelist's Association Elizabeth Goudge writing trophy, is a seasoned tea drinker who writes contemporary and historical family sagas.

Chrissie has always loved match-making a book to a reader. Writing the kind of book she loves to read takes this a step further. When Chrissie is not writing or reading, you will find her walking her dog on the beach, travelling or spending time with her family and friends. She would love to hear from readers.

Chrissie enjoys tweeting on @ChrissieBeee

Her instagram account is chrissie_bradshaw_author

Her blog is www.chrissiebradshaw.com

and she has a Chrissie Bradshaw author page on Facebook.

To join her mailing list, email-
chrissiebradshaw@hotmail.co.uk

ACKNOWLEDGEMENT

I have to thank Rob for encouraging me to write while we were locked down in Spain and our return home to the UK was uncertain. Writing about an epidemic was my way of living through the first months of a pandemic. A special thanks to my wartime recipe tester, Jasmine Tindale-Nixon. I am lucky to have a bunch of supportive friends, too many to mention but you know who you are. Thanks to you all!

Printed in Great Britain
by Amazon

18933881R00072